Escape from Mongolia

Jerry Reid

Published by Oxbow Publishing, 2024.

ESCAPE FROM MONGOLIA

First edition. February 29, 2024.

ISBN: 979-8230239888

Written by Jerry Reid.

Table of Contents

For my mother, Hazel, who was never without a book.
Her unfailing support through all my endeavors was only
matched by her love.

Character List, in order of appearance

Batu Yazdzik – Superb Mongol horseman, adventurer

Shager – Old horseman, observing the horserace

Emlig – Old horseman, observing the horserace

Nyam Gavaa – Grew up with Batu, fellow horseman, friend

George (Geo) Chee – General Tang's sergeant and Udaa Sartaq's lover

Borkay Strazik (Cheech) – Russian prisoner, Willie's guard

Willie Barron – American smuggler in prison with Batu and Nyam

Chong – Nickname for the second Russian prisoner, a traitor

Udaa Sartaq – General Tang's translator, Onar's mother

Saikhan – Willie's cook, murdered by Chong

General Tang – Chinese General, polo enthusiast and scion of the Tang dynasty of world traders

Sin Loc – Chinese prisoner, hostile to all Muslims

Hamid – Innocent Muslim prisoner from Indonesia

Onor Sartaq – Udaa Sartaq's daughter, in love with Nyam

Illia Yorkof – General Tang's Chinese concubine

Major Bagana – Second in command of the prison, greedy

(Sergeant) Tugso Erdene (Uno) – Prison guard, he hates his job

(Sergeant) Rentsen Dorvaa (Dos) – Prison guard, old wrangler

Dorgon (Smiley) – An assassin, tasked to kill

Grandfather Khentii – Old horse trader

Russian from Dansk – Fellow prisoner

Grandfather Rekap – Old man at the water well (pump)

Samantha – The horse "Sam"

Major Khoo – Batu's enemy, responsible for Batu being in prison

Chapter 1
The Race

Batu could hear the pounding hooves and yells of hot pursuit. He steered Tango left with his knees, as he peered at the rough ground ahead. A misstep or slip at this speed, and all would be lost. They were running full-bore across the face of a craggy ridge that could snap a horse's leg like a matchstick. Batu steered left again, a little more uphill. He was worried about treacherous washouts after the recent rains; hazards that were hard to see, and death to a horse at this speed. They crested the ridge, and Batu relaxed a little as they flew down the other side. Suddenly, they were on it — a gully wider than it should have been. He felt Tango leap to clear the gully, but the horse tripped on the other side, and they tumbled headfirst into the rocks. As Batu hit, he heard the dreaded "snap."

END OF SUMMER IN MONGOLIA, and the traditional nomadic tribal games were underway. In the high plains surrounded by mountains, the small village of Sharga was hosting the last summer festival, featuring the foods and games of the nomads who for centuries traveled with their animals, living in yurts and following weather-determined water and grazing. People from neighboring villages cheerfully gathered for the festivities.

Today, there were brutal thirty-kilometer cross-country horse races, called Nadaam, as well as Kok-boru, with men on horseback tossing a headless goat, round and round in a field, like a very rough polo game. With an average elevation of almost a mile, with arid plains, cliffs, craggy mountains, fast streams and washouts, Mongolia was perfect for challenging and grueling horse races, the longest traveling 1000 kilometers. These games, of course, were centered on horses.

Horses were woven into the culture of Mongolia, and the Mongols loved them most of all their livestock. The horses were Roman-nosed, beer-barreled, shaggy, durable, and endowed with the aristocratic name of Piewalski's Horse, given by a Russian nobleman. The Mongol practice of free ranging their horses on the steppes with the wild horses enhanced their bloodlines and durability. They worked their horses, raced them, and grew up riding them. They even ate them, and made a favorite potent drink from fermented mare's milk, called airag.

Today, a fair amount of airag had already been consumed by two wizened old horsemen perched on a high flat rock, offering a good view of the race. The two were elderly and bent, with gnarled hands and bowed legs from years in the saddle. Colorfully dressed in horsehair, fur, colorful wool and leather, they were ready for the cold and for the occasion. Fur-rimmed hats and eagle feathers adorned their long, braided gray hair. Their eyes were sharp, and they were alert and good natured, but were moving slower than usual, for airag did that to you.

Their flat rock was near the mountainous area that had been selected for this racecourse. There were no trees to be seen in the steppes, only grasslands and rocky patches. About fifty people from surrounding villages were gathered on the small promontory for a good view of the approaching riders. The marked trail across the steppes would bring the riders in close.

"Ho!" Shager said, "There's a rider up on the ridge, coming here the hard way. Must be in a hurry to see the racers come by."

Emlig peered at the rider, still a half-mile away. "Yes, he's in a hurry, He's coming straight down that steep ridge. He might lose it."

"Yes, but see how he lays back to help the horse? He's a good rider, and he's big, even from here, almost as big as his horse! Do you suppose it's Nyam Gavaa?" Shager asked.

"He's been gone, you know. Hunting for work, I heard. But look at him play that horse! That's got to be Nyam, alright," Emlig agreed.

The two old horsemen sat on the rock, smiling in appreciation of his horsemanship as they watched Nyam work the horse down the steep grade and begin an easy lope toward them. The horse was lathered up, even in the cold, but pranced a little, like it was enjoying the exercise.

"Goddamn, he's a good horseman," Shager commented.

To the old men's delight, Nyam waved and rode straight towards them, as he nodded hello to other villagers. They waved and smiled, for Nyam was well known.

As he rode up to them, coattails flying, Nyam said, "Whoa! Lock up the women and hide the horses, it's Shager and Emlig!" As everyone laughed, Nyam dipped his head to show respect, and said, "Good morning, grandfathers."

Emlig said, "By the gods, Nyam, you look bigger every time I see you. When are you going to stop growing?"

As Nyam dismounted, his horse whinnied and looked at him as if to say, "Yes, when?" with perfect timing. Nyam shrugged guiltily to his horse, and the crowd roared. It was fun times and comedy in the cold Mongolian air.

Nyam, more seriously, said, "When do you expect the racers to come by? I was afraid I would miss them."

"We heard they would be here in another hour," Shager said, "but you can never tell how far Batu will be out front. Remember last time? He led by almost an hour,"

Emlig, a true student of the sport, shook his head in admiration. "Well, Batu is small and light, but it's more than that. You've seen how he rides forward, leaning down by the horse's neck. And how he talks to them! I've never seen him raise a hand to a horse, and he uses no spurs. But they will do anything for him. It's the damnedest thing."

Nyam was nodding. "You are right, grandfather. I've grown up with Batu, and I believe he communicates with horses in ways we don't know. The horses want to please him."

Shager put his hands on his hips. "Well, you're no slouch on a horse, Nyam, winning all of the Kok-boru goat toss games. The two of you are becoming legendary. You can be proud of yourselves."

Nyam bowed his head at the compliment. With his broad face, slits for eyes, and a naturally downturned mouth, along with his sheer size, it was hard for him to appear humble.

He looked up and said, "You know, Batu and I are fortunate to win these games, but it doesn't put meat in the pot. Work is hard to find now. I've been all the way to Ulan Bator and even South Korea looking for work, and it does not look good."

"My nephew had a job in Korea, putting together cars," Shager said.

"Yes, many Mongols work there, and even learn the language. I went to see for myself, but it was depressing. Small apartments in big buildings jammed together. The air stinks. They eat fish and rice, and there's lots of noise and rules. Our people there were sad and lonely; some have killed themselves. And there are no horses. I did not like Korea."

"Have you talked to Batu lately?" Emlig asked.

"No, Batu and I agreed that I would look far, and he would look near for jobs, and then we would compare notes. Have you seen him?" Nyam asked.

"Yes. Four days ago, I saw Batu at the Little Flower restaurant on the square in the village. I was curious because a new looking Chinese staff car, a Hongqi, was parked in front. And there was Batu, talking to a well-dressed Chinese gentleman. Out of courtesy, Batu introduced me to his guest. His name was Geo Chee. Batu said Mr. Chee may have work for the two of you, and that it involved horses." Emlig smiled, as the bearer of good news, perhaps.

"Chinese? Horses?" Nyam was puzzled. "I wonder what the Chinese are doing here with horses?"

LATER THAT MORNING, the villagers watched, spellbound, as the racers approached. Evenly matched, the riders were bunched up, except for a lone horseman about three-hundred yards in front. The lead horse was running flat-out, ears back, nostrils flared, covered in sweat and grunting with effort at each stride. The horse had a large bleeding gash in its left shoulder.

The rider was Batu Yazdzik. He was sitting strangely in the saddle because of a broken arm. His head gear was gone, and he, and the horse, looked battered.

But as Batu and his horse thundered past the cheering crowd, he gave a high-pitched "Hi-Hi-Hi-Hi-HYAGAHAA!" — a yell of pure joy and abandon, as they continued to outdistance the pack. Batu would win again.

Chapter 2

Two Years Later, Yorbay Prison, Northwest Mongolia

Borkay Strazik, known as "Cheech" to the inmate crew, a huge Mafia killer from Moscow hired to guard Willie Barron's back, awoke with a start in the dark hovel two meters from Willie's door. The lone candle was low, it was dark, and Cheech was confused. Warm water was flooding over him. Where would warm water come from in this frigid place?

Suddenly he smelled it, and he gagged as he realized — Mother of God! — that it was blood flooding down on him, just as Chong, the other monster guard, toppled down on top of him with blood spewing out of his throat. Chong made a gurgling, gasping sound, his body twitching and jerking in death throes. Cheech recognized Batu's knife, the one he used to butcher the horses, a knife he had purchased from a prison guard, sticking out of the center of Chong's throat. He vomited upward into the middle of Chong's face, and saw it drip off Batu's knife handle as he vomited again, then screamed and rolled out from under Chong. Slipping and sliding in the gore, he ran for the open doorway. In his panic, Cheech missed the doorway and ran into the wall, turning over the night bucket, adding yet another odor to the grisly scene.

Cheech finally lurched into the other room, his huge bulk filling the doorway. He stood there covered in blood, vomit and urine, and peered at the diminutive Batu, whose black hair was awry, standing over a water bucket, meticulously washing Chong's blood off of his hands. Somehow, the calm look on Batu's face, as he carefully scrubbed his hands clean, was almost as scary as what Cheech had seen before. It was as if he had just butchered another horse.

Batu turned to Cheech with his black eyes glittering in the candlelight, and asked, "Did you see the garrote in Chong's hands?"

Cheech stood there trembling, and shook his head no. Batu nodded toward the hallway, where Saikhan's yellow boots could be seen.

"He killed Saikhan, and he was quiet about it, but the smell of blood woke me up. He was standing over you with the garrote when I put the knife in him. I think he was going to kill all of us, to get to the stash."

"Mother of God," Cheech barked. "Why would he do this? He was one of us."

Batu nodded again. "Keep your voice down; we don't want to wake up Willie. Chong wanted Willie's stash. As you know, we're all paid very well to keep Willie alive, and everyone wonders where he keeps his money."

Cheech stood in the doorway, looking like a huge specter from a nightmare. He shook his head sadly and said, "Chong should have known. Even though Willie is only an American, he is an experienced smuggler. No one is going to find his stash."

Batu nodded and said, "No, they're not." Then he smiled, indicated the bucket, and asked, "Do you want the rest of this water to wash up with?"

Cheech looked at the little killer for a moment, then nodded and slowly moved toward the bucket.

FINALLY CLEANER AND wrapped in blankets, Cheech began to warm up. When he had recovered a little, they carried the bodies to the pig pens to feed them to the prison guards' hogs. The gory evidence would disappear, and a search would reveal nothing. The prison officials would think the men went over the wall and froze to death in the high desert. As Cheech watched Batu strip the bodies and retrieve his knife, he thought about Batu now, and Batu in the early days. It was an amazing story.

Not only had Batu saved them from Chong, he was also keeping them from starving in this hellhole of a prison. They were living on horsemeat, the "Mongolian delicacy" that was a joke no longer. They were in a day-to-day struggle to stay alive in this prison, located west of Olgii at the borders of China, Mongolia and Russia, not far from Kazakhstan. High in the rugged mountains, it was harsh, cold and desolate.

Ironically named the Yorbay Institute for Reform, the prison was technically a Mongolian institution, due to the nebulous rules governing prisons in Mongolia, and the not-so-nebulous craven desire for a very profitable enterprise. The prison had become the repository for the dregs of society from the four neighboring countries, plus other misplaced ne'er do wells. The Yorbay Institute for Reform, called URBAD by everyone, was a dangerous place. Mostly, the guards "patrolled" the grounds from their warm huts on the stockade walls, leaving the prisoners to govern themselves. They were starving, because prison food, supplies and equipment were diverted by prison officials to the black markets. Even the prison hogs were only for the benefit of the guards and officials, though the prisoners were required to tend them. Men could freeze to death at this altitude, with few blankets or fuel for the fires. The huts were drafty.

Within the stockade walls, the prisoners had to fend for themselves. Death and dismemberment were common occurrences, and the prison officials could care less. The prison was a dark, dirty place, where there were few rules, and it was every man for himself. And with desperate inmates from such diverse backgrounds, you could die at the hands of your neighbors at any time and for no reason. It was the worst collection of murderers, thieves, deserters, rapists, perverts and sadists that you could imagine, many of whom claimed to be innocent. Life was very cheap at URBAD.

BATU HAD BECOME A LEGEND in the prison by disappearing for twelve days upon his arrival, after his first horrifying look at the mean, hungry and perverted eyes of the prison inmates — the dregs of society for sure. He knew that to survive, he would have to disappear, and disappear he did. One moment he was standing there among the new prisoners — and the next moment he was gone. No one had seen him move.

While Batu was hidden, the prison officials searched the entire facility and questioned each inmate. Every day the mystery grew, as no one knew where the new prisoner had gone. Officials finally threatened torture for all prisoners unless Batu turned himself in to them. By loudspeaker, they promised immunity from his "desertion" and a safe haven from his surroundings if he presented himself in the yard before noon the next day. Furthermore, they announced, if Batu did <u>not</u> show up at the appointed time, all of the prisoners would be severely punished every day he remained absent — because obviously the prisoners were hiding him.

As the reporting hour neared, speculation and bets soared. Was he dead from the severe cold and no food for all this time? What condition would he be in, if he showed up? And the prisoners were worried. There was no doubt that the punishment threat would be carried out. Prison officials were very upset by the whole affair, and felt they were being made fools. Tensions were running high all over the camp.

On the twelfth day of Batu's disappearance (which was Friday the thirteenth), the prisoners were assembled in the prison yard at gunpoint and in ranks, in preparation for the punishment to come if Batu did not appear. The favored punishment was the "gauntlet" to be run by each prisoner between two lines of prison guards. The guards loved the gauntlet. It was an opportunity to settle old scores and relieve tension, using rifle stocks, pick handles, and even bayonets. Usually, some prisoners did not survive the gauntlet, and the guards had no need to worry about recrimination — after all, the prisoner was "struck down while running." It looked good on paper.

As the appointed hour approached, the tension rose higher and higher. Not only were many bets on the table, but an element of real fear existed because of the gauntlet. The prisoners stood in ranks under the guards' guns. They were allowed to stamp their feet because of the freezing cold, but if they moved out of ranks, they would be shot. They were underfed, emaciated, scared and freezing, their breath coming in great plumes in the frigid air. Near twelve noon, movement in the ranks stopped. Even the guards quit moving. It became quiet in the yard. There was a feeling of desperation in the air. Then there was silence, everyone was listening and watching, almost forgetting their own misery. More silence, and one of the sick prisoners started a low keening sound of despair. Then everyone heard it at once, a light crunching sound in the snow. They dared not look, or even hope, as the measured crunching sound grew nearer. Then they saw him, a slight figure wearing a horse-blanket poncho, with rags around his head against the cold.

He looked in good condition — not starved at all — as he marched up to the guard commander and presented a snappy military salute. In a clear voice he stated, "Private Batu Yazdzik, reporting as ordered, sir."

Absolute pandemonium broke out all over the prison.

With loud cheering and backslapping, ranks were broken as the laughing prisoners collected bets from each other and expressed relief that they had dodged the gauntlet. The guards stared at Batu in amazement. He was in good condition, better than most of the prisoners. No starvation, no frostbite. Where had he been and how had he done this? They had been through the prison so many times and had watched the prisoners carefully since the disappearance. They knew he had no help from the inside.

As the prisoners chattered and moved back to their hovels to escape the cold, Batu was grabbed by the guards and thrown in "the box" for beatings, questioning, and torture. The promises that had been made meant nothing.

During his brutal interrogation, Batu made one statement, and he said it only once, as they worked him over.

"Sirs, with all due respect, I cannot tell you where I went, because I may need to go there again."

This strange answer had a mystic quality, and as word of it leaked to the yard, it served to enhance Batu's aura of the supernatural.

The poor, miserable, starving and ever-suffering prisoners had something to think about, which for the moment, elevated them from the numbing misery of the camp. They speculated endlessly about Batu's statement: "I may need to go there again." What did that mean? Could Batu fly over the walls? Why hadn't he starved to death in all those days? Was he magic?

As Batu's beatings continued into the second day, a strange thing happened. Although no word was passed, the prisoners, all of them, started gathering at the entryway to "the box" where Batu was held. Not a word was said, they just stood in the freezing cold and waited, looking at the door. Prison officials were unnerved by this whole affair. This eerie silent gathering of the prisoners broke their resolve to further punish Batu. It was strange to them how, as the beatings continued, Batu never said another word. It was almost as if he was waiting for something. They did not know how to handle this, so they turned Batu loose, passing him brutally out the door to the waiting prisoners.

Batu, barely conscious, did not understand what was happening. He knew he was broken up. Both feet and an arm were broken, his face was lacerated, and he had deep bruises all over his body. He hurt all over, and he was being carried gently across the prison yard by the same prisoners that had terrified him. But he felt safe, because they were chanting, "Batu! Batu!", and touching him lightly, as if for good luck. The truth was that Batu would never come to harm by any of the prisoners, ever. He had beaten the prison system with style, dignity, and perhaps a little magic. He was their hero.

LATER, BATU BECAME more of a hero, but in the early days his survival was a very close thing. The American smuggler, Willie Barron, took charge of the Mongolian's care and feeding. It was not all generosity on Willie's part. As a born smuggler, subversion was his business. Willie wanted to know how Batu did his "hat trick," disappearing for twelve days, then reappearing.

Batu's status in the prison contributed to his recovery. Prisoners shared their meager morsels of food, when they themselves were hungry, to help assure his survival. Batu never forgot the generosities that were given, but vowed to repay them ten-fold, and he did.

He lay for months in "Willie's Compound," trying to get his broken feet and arm to heal. The bruises were deep, and he had some internal injuries. His feet would forever hurt when he walked, causing him to have a slight "mincing" step.

But the little Mongolian healed and was glad to be alive. He spent many hours lying on his stomach with his broken feet sticking up (less pain), playing draw poker with Willie and his crew. Willie's hut was warmed by a crude stove, and guarded by prisoners he trusted, making for a calm oasis. Willie, a master smuggler, had money and contraband delivered to the prison in a number of ingenious ways.

As time went by and Batu healed, he became very good at poker, much to Willie Barron's chagrin. Batu began building his own stash out of his winnings. He was also improving his Russian with Cheech and Chong and learning English from Willie.

Finally, back on his feet, Batu roamed the yard, talking to prisoners and thanking them. He could see they were starving, many were sick, and there was not enough firewood and blankets to stay warm. There were fewer fights and killings, but still many deaths from sickness and some suicides.

Willie Barron, the drug smuggler, and Batu, the Mongolian private, engaged in long conversations. They were an interesting pair. Batu was small, of slight stature, with black hair that seemed to sprout out in all directions. He had very black obsidian-like eyes that seemed to glow in his head and were very observant — those black eyes missed nothing. He was quiet, intelligent and had a knack for languages. Willie Barron, a tenacious extrovert, was of medium height and thin with a narrow bony head. His light blue eyes peered out like cut crystals. He was a born thief and smuggler.

Willie wanted to know Batu's hat trick. He would ask, "How did you survive twelve days hidden in this hellhole, and step out into the daylight looking like you just took a walk in the park?" Batu would never say, but would change the subject by asking about the smuggling business or poker strategy.

In their discussions, Willie could tell that Batu had something on his mind, and he kept probing until things started to happen. "Come on, tell me what you're planning. Another disappearance?"

Batu sighed, leaned back, and said, "I propose that we pool some of 'our' money and do some things to make life better in this camp, and at the same time, I will show you, if you are patient and pay attention, how was done the hat trick." Then Batu added, "Also maybe help you play better poker."

Willie, wanting to know Batu's secret hiding place, had nursed Batu back to health. Despite himself, they became friends. Willie learned that Batu was a strategist and tactician. Though they had played many hours of poker and worked to improve life in the prison, he still didn't know Batu's secret.

Batu further enhanced his status by engineering a free-range horse wrangling operation outside the prison walls that provided horsemeat for the prisoners. He convinced the officials to allow him out, under loose guard, to collect wild horses, which could be butchered to feed the prisoners. The officials would have first pick, profiting from this new prison resource. Because he was providing food for the whole prison, Batu was allowed to carry a knife and run a "horse processing" operation. Besides eating the horses, their hides were used for footwear and blankets, the manes for rope and thread. Batu was gold in the prison. Seen as a hero and a savior, no one would harm him, even when he took their money at poker. Life in the prison eased a bit, as both inmates and guards benefited from the improvements.

NOW GATHERED AROUND the tiny stove in Willie's hovel, recuperating from the recent murder and mayhem, Willie "the Goat" Barron was pissed off. The American drug smuggler, so nick-named because of the unfortunate lack of bridge to his nose, was upset because of the loss of his cook.

"Goddamn it, Batu," Willie said, "Saikhan was the best horsemeat cook in URBAD, and you let Chong kill him!"

"Chong was going to kill you, too," Batu pointed out.

"What does it matter?" Willie said, "Now I'll starve to death with a sub-standard cook." He wailed on, "Saikhan had a talent. He could make horsemeat taste like filet mignon."

Cheech, still covered in a blanket, pointed a huge bony finger at Willie and said, "Willie, you should remember when we didn't even have horses to eat, before Batu came along with his horse rustling ways."

Willie grinned, seeing the humor of the situation. "Maybe we should have eaten Chong instead of feeding him to the warden's fucking hogs."

Batu laughed. "Cannibalism is against the law." They all laughed, releasing the tension of almost being killed by one of their own.

Sitting in silence, trying to stay warm, the three were lost in their own thoughts. Willie, for the millionth time, cursed himself for getting careless years ago, while checking his drug supply lines too close to the Chinese border. The Chinese bastards actually came across the border for him, and he ended up in this hellhole.

Cheech thought about Chong. What caused him to betray his mates? They had worked together for years. Wasn't the money he got from Willie enough?

Batu prayed for the horses he loved. He asked forgiveness for the many horses that died at his hands, again, and again, and again.

They all broke the silence at about the same time, saying almost in unison, "We've got trouble."

It stood to reason, and Willie voiced it first. "Chong would never do what he did without help. First, he killed my cook who was guarding the door. Then he moved on to Cheech, opening the way, not knowing that Batu was back."

Batu nodded. He had returned early from a poker game with two guards and an Afghan prisoner and had laid along the wall on a blanket near the stove rather than going to his bunk.

Cheech said to Willie, "With me dead, and thinking Batu was gone, Chong could unbolt the door for a clear path to the back room where you sleep." Cheech rubbed his bald, scarred head, looked down the hallway, and said, "They think your stash is in your crib."

Willie summed it up succinctly. "We, my friends, are hanging by a thread. I can almost feel the tension through the walls. They are coming for us."

Batu, ever the tactician, said, "We need to make a statement."

Willie gave a cynical laugh, while Cheech grinned.

"What you mean, is we need to kill some people," Willie said.

Hunching his shoulders, Cheech asked reasonably, "But how do we know who to kill?"

SO THEY CAME UP WITH a plan. A plan that would flush out the attackers, deal with them properly, and put to bed the prevalent theory that the stash was somewhere in Willie's bunk area. But they were short of one element to pull the plan off, and Willie and Batu discussed it at length.

Willie chewed on a straw, leaned back on his bunk, and looked at the ceiling as he spoke, "You know it's a good plan, but you know who we need to pull it off?"

Batu answered as he sharpened his knife, "I know who you are thinking of, but he's been our eyes in the yard, so to speak. We have been safer with him quietly watching our back."

"Batu, my friend," Willie grinned, "if we don't take care of this now, there aren't going to be any backs to watch. Those fuckers are circling us like a pack of wolves."

Batu looked up from his knife. "Okay, but if we call Nyam Gavaa in, I'm going to want something from you. Something big."

Willie looked at Batu with a look of disappointment. "Batu, are you getting greedy?"

Batu smiled and said, "This isn't about money, Willie, it's about love."

Willie shook his head, as he waved his hand to signal that the meeting was over. "What the hell are you talking about, Batu? There's no love within a thousand miles of this place."

SO THEY LAUNCHED THE plan. To start with, Nyam Gavaa was spirited out of the yard, and held "waiting in the wings", so to speak. Private Gavaa had grown up with Batu Yazdzik in the Altai Mountains of northeastern Mongolia. Improbably, both Mongols, being excellent horsemen, had been recruited into China's People's Liberation Army by Brigadier General Tang, primarily to play polo. Tang, very competitive, would go anywhere for good polo players. He even had a German on the team.

But both Mongols ran afoul of the Chinese Army, and strangely, both ended up in this remote prison that was essentially a dumping ground for castaways. Batu had struck an officer whose stupidity on a self-propelled gun had caused the death of a loader, and Nyam had caused an international incident. Nyam's reconnaissance patrol on the China/Russia border had strayed into Russian territory and were chased back toward the Chinese border by Russian Infantry. The Russians became discouraged in their pursuit when they realized that Nyam was doubling back on them, collecting Russian heads and leaving them along the trail. They never saw the bodies. As Russia and China were not at war, the affair caused an international incident and Nyam was sent to jail for barbarism to appease the Russians.

NYAM GAVAA, A LARGE dark-eyed mountain of a man, moved very lightly on his feet for a big man. His head was bald, he had little ears, and his eyes peered through mere slits in his Oriental face. His most striking feature was his smile, which didn't resemble a smile at all, but rather a grimace. With his reputation, when he looked at you and smiled, he was scary. Those around him would rather he did not smile. Nyam was a good person to have at your back.

With Nyam hidden in Willie's crib, the next step in the plan was carried out. They organized a poker tournament in the yard. It was a big event, and almost everyone attended. Those not playing were watching and betting; much money, markers and cigarettes were changing hands. Card games in the yard had become a regular event, when the weather permitted. Poker was the game of choice; its intricacies having migrated into the prison years ago via the international mix of the prisoners. Even the guards played in some games and were a good source of new money, as well as news from the outside. The players in the yard were indeed a colorful crowd, with about every ethnic mix you could imagine. Some played with scraps of paper that served as cards. The prisoners' hovels, though locked, were unattended.

As the card play proceeded, Willie and his crew were very cautious, watching each other's backs. Batu won steadily, as usual.

Suddenly, there was yelling as someone realized Willie's hovel was on fire, the whole building engulfed in flames, with black smoke billowing out and up and the stench of burning flesh. A bucket brigade was formed to wet down the adjacent buildings. The prison guards were doubled, suspecting a diversion for a breakout.

Willie's hovel burned down to mere embers. As the building smoked, the bodies of three big Russian inmates from Dansk could be seen draped over the remains of Willie's bunk. The message was very clear: the stash was not in Willie's hovel, and it was best not to mess with Willie Barron and his crew.

As the fire was finally extinguished, the guards swarmed the prisoners with rifles and bayonets, beating them and forcing them into the center of the yard. A headcount was taken, and prisoners were interrogated to determine what had happened. The guards feared escape or revolt, and were relieved to learn the dead were Russians — a group that had been a lot of trouble. The guards hated them.

So, incredibly, Willie and his crew were given the Russian's hovel, and Nyam's battered condition was attributed to the recent beatings handed out by the guards.

Willie shook his head, smiled and said, "Man, when you're lucky, you're lucky."

"This is a better location, I like the view," joked Willie as they moved into the recently-deceased's quarters.

Cheech grinned, as he had finally found a bunk long enough for him to stretch out. But Batu was not happy. Nyam, his lifelong friend, was hunched over in the corner, coughing up blood, his arm hanging awkwardly.

NYAM, AS PART OF THE plan, had been waiting for the intruders as they came into Willie's hovel. The three Russians, using the distraction of the card games, had snuck into Willie's hut to rifle through his bunk. With his tremendous strength, Nyam had arched himself along the open ceiling in the darkness and dropped on the three big men like a catamount. He managed to kill all three of them, using Batu's knife and a hay fork hidden nearby.

Knowing he would be outnumbered, Nyam had planned the fight well. He had placed the hayfork with the tines pointing upward, like the pikes used against charging horses by Roman infantry. However, it worked almost too well. As Nyam dropped on the Russians, drawing them forward onto the pitchfork tines, he was pierced in the side by the tines going all the way through the first Russian. The second Russian was dead, his throat cut as Nyam went by with Batu's razor-sharp knife.

This left the third Russian untouched, and very healthy. It was a bloody one-on-one fight in close quarters, in the dark, between two big men. The big Russian was more than a match for the bleeding Nyam, whose arm was broken during the last exchange of blows.

Encouraged, the Russian lunged viciously at Nyam in the dark, but crashed into the end of Willie's bunk, crushing his Adam's apple and cutting off his air. As the Russian choked and died in the dark, Nyam lay on the floor, bleeding, but relieved, and said to himself, *"I'll take luck, anytime."* But the brutal fight left him suffering with internal injuries, a hole in his side, and a broken arm.

Even with his injuries, Nyam had carried out the last of the plan. He piled the bodies onto Willie's bunk and set them on fire. Mission complete, but he was the worse for wear.

NOW, BATU NEGOTIATED with Willie, with a hard look in his eye that Willie had not seen before.

"Willie," Batu said, "I want you to buy Nyam out of here."

Willie was aghast. "What do you think, I'm made of money?" Then Willie looked at Nyam and said, "Looks like he's going to die anyway. Although I appreciate the job that he's done." He shook his head. "We've even got nice new quarters."

"I know how we can get him out, and with your help, we can do it. This is serious," Batu said.

"What do you mean, serious?" Willie asked. These were words he and Batu had never used when negotiating.

"What I mean is," Batu said, "this is about love."

"Jesus Christ, there's that word again," Willie yelled, wondering why the word upset him so much. "What the hell do you mean, love?" Willie asked.

"Nyam misses his woman. He loves her, and she needs him." Batu stated. "Getting him out will save them both."

Willie was taken aback, and frankly, touched. He had not even thought of such emotions in such a long time. All of this put him a little off-kilter and affected his negotiating skills. Batu was never easy to negotiate with. It reminded him of the old saying about what you had to check for when you got up from the table after hard negotiations: *"Be sure you still have your watch, wallet, spectacles and testicles!"* Willie was concerned he was about to lose the latter, the only thing on the list he still had.

"What we do is," Batu said earnestly, "We buy Nyam out of this godforsaken place, and into the Mongolian Army. We hide him in plain sight."

"What?" Willie yelled. "Are you out of your mind? He's already in the fucking <u>Chinese</u> Army!"

Willie didn't like the sound of this. It was going to cost him money. Buy this, buy that, Batu was out of his mind, and what's love got to do with it?

Batu smiled, "I've been playing cards with some of the Mongolian officers, part of the guard detail."

"And?" Willie asked, waiting for the other shoe to drop.

"Nyam and I no longer exist on the Chinese Army rolls. This prison is a dumping ground, and no one is expected to return."

"And?" Willie asked again, dreading Batu's logic.

"So, we can buy Nyam into the Mongolian Army, cover his tracks perfectly, and he will be free to be with his woman. The Mongolian Army needs veterans, especially with Nyam's skills in reconnaissance."

Willie knew that Batu's logic was sound. Willie had served in the Marine Corps with Germans, Canadians and Poles that were not citizens of the U.S. Many joined to fast-track their path to U.S. citizenship. Their backgrounds were checked, and they had to take an oath. But once they were Marines, these foreigners melted into the ranks, and no one paid attention to their past. The Germans had been handy to do the heavy lifting. Batu's idea would work. After all, Nyam was a Mongol already. What difference did it make that he had served in the Chinese Army? Who would know that he had been in prison?

"Yeah, the Russians will just have a head-rolling shit when they hear he's on the loose," Willie grumbled.

"Willie, the Russians and the Chinese will not know Nyam is out. He will just be another Mongolian soldier. And the good news is, I'm holding some gambling markers on these officers and gentlemen, which will reduce the cost of buying Nyam out," Batu reasoned.

"So, what is buying Nyam out of prison and into the Mongolian Army going to cost?" Willie asked. Shit. Batu was all caught up in this love thing and it was going to cost him a fortune.

Batu broke into an uncharacteristic wide smile, "With my markers going into the deal, we will only need an additional twenty-five thousand dollars, U.S. money."

Willie dipped his head and looked over at the suffering Nyam. Maybe it would be okay if he didn't die after all. And since he had quietly guarded their backs for years, maybe he deserved to see his woman.

Willie sat back, sighed and said, "Shit, Batu, I thought it was going to cost <u>real</u> money. That's nothing. Go for it."

Chapter 3
Bird Hotels and Love

Weeks later, an uncharacteristic warm spell occurred, and a blanket of small, blue, fragile-looking flowers bloomed inside of the prison walls, right under the guards' guns. The prisoners looked at the small flowers with appreciation and mixed thoughts. Some were awed by the beauty and fragility of these beautiful little flowers in such a hellhole as this. Others thought of times past, when they witnessed flowers such as these in a young girl's hair, and they almost wept.

Willie's crew lay in the sunshine, around a brazier, slowly roasting strips of horsemeat, turned occasionally over the manure-fed flames. Cheech was in his favorite position, flat on his back, legs spread, arms out, looking through his eyelids at nothing, occasionally nodding as though having secret thoughts. Nyam was the cook today, tending the fire, turning the meat, stooped over from his wounds but recovering quickly. Batu was relaxed against the wall, looking at the flowers with a thousand-yard stare. It was plain to see that he had something on his mind, other than the horrifying events of yesterday. Willie was unusually quiet, thinking of what happened and trying to come up with a way to cheer up his crew.

It had started as a cruel joke, carried out by Sin Loc, a huge Chinese prisoner that took delight in persecuting Hamid, a Muslim prisoner. Hamid loved his Indonesian country of Kalimantan, and would tell stories of his town, Kumai, on the river of the same name. He told of the hundred-foot-long Indonesian freighters that plied the Kumai River, with their ancient swayback designs, strange outboard rudders and slanted pilot houses, built of a special wood that lasted five hundred years in saltwater. Hamid spoke of the orangutans, roaming the jungle just across the river, east of town. He loved Kumai, and described the beautiful mosques, of which there were over forty in his town. He spoke of dawn in Kumai, when the muezzins would start the first calls to prayers, on loudspeakers on the mosques all over the city, and how the cacophony of all the unsynchronized calls at once made a very special music to his ears. There were many weddings that spilled into the narrow streets, and Hamid told them how the arak flowed, the mothers-in-law roamed, good food was everywhere, and karaoke singing was the main entertainment. Hamid also talked of Islam, and how any Muslim could go to any mosque and find sanctuary there. He was a fine religious man who, being at the wrong place at the wrong time, ended up in this hellhole. He was a prisoner who was truly innocent.

Perhaps because of Hamid's piety, Sin Loc tormented him at every opportunity. He would grab Hamid with his left (unclean) hand, uncover Hamid's head, and show the bottom of his feet to Hamid. He would step on Hamid's prayer rug when it was out for prayer. And finally, only yesterday, Sin Loc's masterpiece — he had found a large rabbit's foot (for luck), so large that it looked like it had great potential.

Sim Loc approached Hamid as he was eating small chunks of horsemeat, threw the rabbit's foot down in front of him and yelled, "How do you like the dog meat? We just cut it up for you." And he laughed, and laughed, and laughed.

Hamid, terrified that, as a Muslim, he had just eaten one of the most unclean of animals, jumped up, and ran screaming through the prison yard, past all the inmates that looked at him in wonder, and straight past the "deadline." The deadline, created during the American Civil War to restrict captured prisoners without adequate prison facilities, and now popular in prisons, was a line drawn in the yard beyond which one did not go, under penalty of immediate death.

And so it was, that Hamid, the gentle religious Muslim, was gunned down before the eyes of the yard population.

Sin Loc showed no remorse whatsoever. He laughed and strolled back to his hovel, telling jokes to his comrades.

EVEN NOW, BATU'S THOUSAND-yard stare swept past the beautiful flowers, to Hamid's grave by the wall, and a tear trickled down his cheek. The grave should not have been near the wall, but the prisoners had insisted and prevailed.

Sin Loc was no more. Batu had paid him a visit in the middle of the night, moving like a ghost through the crowded hut. An avenging angel, he cut the Chinaman's throat with a piece of broken glass, not wanting to desecrate his knife on such scum. As many horses as he had killed, murdering the fat Chinaman was easy, almost too easy. Batu was getting tired of this place.

Reclining in the sunshine, Willie was puzzling over the reporting dates along one of his supply lines. The island of Trinidad, ten time zones away, always reported sooner than Lagos, Nigeria, only six time zones away. Very confusing. Was time lost due to transmission delays? He had no idea, and his "messengers" had no explanation. Trying to figure it out, Willie was distracted by the listlessness of his crew. Hamid's unexpected death had them reeling. Although hardened against cruelty and death, the killing of the innocent Muslim had them all depressed. He needed to shake them out of it. Then Willie had a revelation — he would tell a story to cheer up his crew.

Willie looked at Batu, who was still staring at the flowers and Hamid's grave. "Batu, you ever hear of Bird Hotels?"

Batu slowly looked up, his shoulders still slumped, and asked, disinterestedly, "What? Bird Hotels?"

"Yeah," Willie continued, "Bird Hotels. Any of you guys ever hear of Bird Hotels? Saw them first when I was in Indonesia on business, not far from where Hamid was from."

Nyam twisted his head curiously, as he peered through the smoking meat on the fire and said, "Bird Hotels? Hotels for birds?" The thought sounded ridiculous.

Cheech raised his head, looked at Willie like he was crazy, but didn't bother to say anything.

"Yup," Willie said, "Bird Hotels. Big business."

Batu was getting curious despite himself. "What is a Bird Hotel?" he asked.

Willie grinned; he had set the hook. He said, "You guys ever hear of bird's nest soup? Well, there's never enough nests to go around. You see, the Chinese are bananas for bird nest soup, which is made from real bird nests that are held together with bird spit. They love the stuff and pay big money for bird's nest soup. It's a delicacy."

Willie saw that they were not quite buying the Bird Hotel thing, even though, having been stationed in China, Batu and Nyam knew about the soup.

Willie continued, sounding like an authority on Chinese culture, which he definitely was not. "There aren't enough nests to gather from the cliffs anymore, and food is a very big deal to the Chinese. Their standard greeting isn't 'What's going on, dude?' or 'Yo, bro,' they will say, 'Have you eaten lately?' Way back, some of their young actually grew up on dog's milk. Food is a very big deal to millions of Chinese, so they build Bird Hotels."

This, from an over-the-hill, ex-marine, drug dealer and smuggler, and now suddenly a Chinese Cultural Expert. Willie's crew shook their heads, but they were still listening.

Willie continued his story, despite the apparent skepticism.

"What they do is, they block off the windows of old buildings, leaving holes for ventilation and enough light to attract the right birds, who build nests in the sanctuaries. These are harvested for bird nest soup, an expensive delicacy, worth big bucks. Some of my suppliers have even started building them."

By this time, Willie was waving his hands, and erecting grand hotels in the air, for birds to flock in by the dozens. The guards looked down at him curiously, wondering perhaps if he was coming down with something, or got religion?

Willie continued, "So these Chinese friends of mine built up this bird hotel, trying to get everything right. But the birds are slow to arrive, and most of them fly straight through the hotel, they don't stop to build a nest."

"My friends discuss this at length. The ventilation looks right; not too stuffy. The light is good. The approach and departure paths are clear. What is the problem?"

"So, they call in a consultant, who sells them two tape recordings to play, one of birds arriving in the evening to roost, and another of birds departing in the morning to begin their day. My Chinese friends are excited, and they station themselves at the entrance to the hotel and at the exit, abacuses clicking, counting the birds. Hoping that more will arrive than depart, indicating that they are nesting. But the birds come, then leave. No birds are nesting. The tapes are not working."

"They call the bird consultant back in. They want their money back. Their Bird Hotel is still empty. They are tired of counting birds coming, and then leaving the hotel."

"The consultant is puzzled. 'It's always worked before,' he grouses. He studies the layout, checks the humidity and ventilation, and watches the birds. He has them play the tapes, then he looks incredulously at the guys and says, 'You idiots, you got the tapes switched! You are confusing the birds!'"

"My friends switch the tapes, and the arriving birds are happy and settle in to nest. In the morning, the proper tape is played, and the birds depart. More birds arrived the next evening. Soon the Bird Hotel had a full profitable occupancy!"

By this time, Willie's crew was laughing, rolling in the dirt. Nyam's grin/grimace was wide, looking like he was sitting on something painful. The "bummer" spell was broken, and Willie's crew was back on keel. Willie went back to worrying about his outside businesses.

THE WEATHER CONTINUED to improve, warmer and sunnier. The little blue flowers were now growing on Hamid's grave. For no apparent reason in this hellhole, there was a feeling of optimism in the air. The card games were more spirited, and even the horsemeat tasted a little better.

Willie was now sporting a single braid in his beard. The braid hung down about six inches, and he had affixed a red ribbon at the end of the braid, hanging down like a small kite tail. With his unbridged nose, close-together eyes, bony narrow face, and now the braid, Willie looked more like a goat than ever. Willie's friends looked at him askance; and wondered at this strange new behavior.

Willie spent a lot of time putting together a plan for Nyam's departure. Timing and treachery were but two of the problems. It was agreed that one half of the money would be paid up front to two compromised URBAD wall guards and their supervisor. These individuals had agreed to transport Nyam to Dalandzadgad in southern Mongolia, where, with the help of bribes, Nyam would enlist in the Mongolian Army. Willie felt that the treacherous guards would simply kill Nyam and roll him over in a ditch, but for the other half of the money, which would be paid when Nyam arrived safely. Timing was a problem because of the distance to be traveled and the condition of the springtime roads. Willie feared that the guards would become impatient for the money, and they had the guns.

Willie explained, "Dalandzadgad is two time zones away. The roads can get mired in mud from the rains, and bridges can wash out by raging rivers with the snow melt. It could take weeks for Nyam to arrive, and longer to get a message back to us. Our guard friends will become very impatient for the rest of the money. We may need to deal with that."

Willie sat on the floor of his hovel, his back to the wall, his elbows on his knees, his head swinging back and forth as he spoke, the pigtail on his beard with the red ribbon swinging like a metronome.

"Nyam," Willie asked, "tell me more about this woman, that's causing you, and now the rest of us, to jump through our asses like this."

Nyam tried to smile, gave it up, and answered, "She is not my wife yet, but I have known her for years, even though she is just now only seventeen years."

Willie was astonished. "What? You've only known her as a little girl?"

Nyam, ignoring Willie's outburst, continued. "Her name is Onor. She is the daughter of Udaa Sartaq, the Mongolian translator hired by General Tang to help us learn Chinese in the early days when we played polo in Chengdu. Udaa is from Dalandzadgad, she learned Chinese and English in a missionary school. When we were not in the field on maneuvers or playing polo, we gathered at Illia Yorkof's villa, owned by General Tang. Illia was Tang's concubine, a wonderful person, and she treated us like her children. 'Nyam,' she would say, 'are you eating enough?' The polo team had great fellowship at Illia's villa. We ate well, we played cards, and we told great stories, and we learned Chinese and English. General Tang was a good host as well as polo team leader. We had very happy times hanging out at the villa."

With a dreamy look, Nyam went on, "And Onor, the translator's daughter, was there at the villa with us in those times. She was just a young girl, and, for some reason, she was fond of me. She called me 'Nyam Bear,' and followed me around like a puppy. Onor would always sit near to me at the card games and meals. And she would go into the fields, draw pictures of wildflowers, and present them to me. She was very cute. She had an open face, beady little black eyes, hair in all directions, and always a great smile. She would say 'Nyam Bear, did you miss me?' even though I had seen her just hours before. She was really small, and she walked forward on the balls of her feet with little steps, swinging her hands back and forth at her sides, looking up at me with that smile."

"Then I left for the Russian border, to do reconnaissance along the Amir River, and I never saw her again."

Nyam stared at the floor of the hovel, listened to the rain beating on the leaky roof, and looked at the various pots and cups catching the drips in the sleeping area. This was the most he had ever spoken. He was embarrassed that he told all of this to Willie. How he was powerfully drawn to a little girl that he had never touched. He felt the need to explain further.

"Willie, the new prisoner from Dalandzadgad said the inmates there spoke of a young woman who pestered the guards about a prisoner named Nyam. She would approach the prison walls almost daily and ask the guards if they had heard of a large prisoner named Nyam Gavaa, if they could tell her if he was still alive. She said she needed to get a message to this Nyam."

"You see, Willie," Nyam anguished, "They fear we are dead, and that there is no hope. And that is why I must jump through my ass, as you say, to go to Onor."

Willie "The Goat" Barron, drug dealer and smuggler extraordinaire, left the hut without a word and walked toward the stables, deep in thought. He was thinking about Nyam's story. Willie was deeply touched by Onor's love for "Nyam Bear." This was a thing he could hardly get his mind around. Willie could never remember anyone caring for him in that way. It was a priceless gift to receive.

WILLIE BECAME MORE reclusive, spending most of his time in his bunk, talking to himself. The crew carried on as usual but watched over him carefully. They were concerned that he was having a mental breakdown.

After three days of this strange behavior, Willie called the crew together. Standing before them like he was making a formal declaration, he looked at each one of the crew, his head to one side, as if he was concentrating.

Then he said, "Gentlemen, I apologize for my behavior these past days. Let me explain. I have had the melancholies, brought on by the realization that much has been lost. Nyam's story about Onor's love for him made me aware that there is more to life than gaining ground in battles. I've always cursed the generals that caused the loss of a lot of good men — the French generals thinking their infantry's "elan" could overcome German machine guns; the English underestimating the Turks at Gallopoli; my own venerated General Robert E. Lee ordering Pickett's charge; even USMC's Chesty Puller, willing to trade a truckload of dog tags to capture a hill. So many good men were lost to poor decisions by generals."

Willie continued, "You know, I've always thought about lost battles, lost ground, lost money, lost business opportunities, and so on; but Nyam made me realize there's more to life than winning battles. Nyam is willing to risk his life for something I've honestly never thought about — the gaining of a good woman's love. I think it's something we should all keep in mind — that's a battle we don't want to lose."

"In the meantime," Willie grinned, "we need to get Nyam Gavaa back to civilization, and to his Onor."

Chapter 4
Nyam's Escape Plan

Ironically, even as Willie "the Goat" Barron and his crew spoke of Nyam's escape, far above them, up on the prison wall, the very same subject was being discussed. The two URBAD sergeants-of-the-guard who generally ran the security on the wall were known to Willie's crew as "Uno" and "Dos" because of the huge Mexican-gunfighter-type moustaches they favored. The two Mongolians were discussing life in general, and Nyam's "escape" in particular.

Sergeant Uno, a big man with sad eyes and a large, hooked nose, twitching his huge moustache, began, "I hate this damn job." He sniffed the smell of the latrines, just upwind. "All we do is sit on this wall, waiting to shoot those poor bastards if they cross the deadline. We do hardly anything else, and the less we do, the less we want to do. We are growing lazy and fat. Did I say I hate this damn job?"

Sergeant Dos laughed at Uno's outburst, nodding his bushy head in agreement. "Yes, I hear you, my friend, but you must admit, the job is sometimes profitable. When we get Nyam over the wall, we'll make a 'chunk of change' as the American says."

Uno nodded, "Yeah, but sadly, we will only get half the cash. I'm sure the Major will kill him outside the wall. At only twelve thousand plus, there's not enough cash in this deal for such a long journey. Nyam's a dead man walking."

Dos agreed, "Yeah. The Major's main goal was to get rid of these gambling markers held by Batu. It's a matter of face, an honorable way to eliminate the debt."

Then Dos asked, "How does Batu win at cards all the time, anyway? It's like he can see through the cards!"

Uno motioned for them to move further down the wall, away from the latrines, and said, "I know one thing for sure, I'm not going to play cards with that little Mongolian fuck anymore."

EVEN AS THE GUARDS spoke, down in the yard a rousing card game was underway. Willie held a very good poker hand for once, and anticipated bumping the pot for a nice win, when Batu folded.

"Goddamn it, Batu," Willie yelled, "How come every time I get a good hand, you turn your cards down? Are you marking the deck?"

Batu smiled, "Willie, it's a new deck that you just smuggled in. How could I mark a new deck?"

Willie looked at the two sergeants up on the wall, across the yard. It was almost as if he was clairvoyant about their recent conversation. He looked at them thoughtfully, and unconsciously twitched his upper lip as he considered the situation. Willie had been doing this lip thing a lot lately, to the point where the men around him were doing the same affectation. Batu, who saw everything, thought maybe they were all going crazy.

In the interest of sanity and continued good will, Batu decided to confess about the cards.

"Willie," Batu said, "my winning at cards has to do with horses."

Willie was incredulous, "Horses?" Then he twitched his upper lip.

Cheech, also sitting at the table, unconsciously twitched his lip. Nyam, across from Cheech, also lifted his lip, but with his face, it looked like a real nerve problem. Batu saw all of those lips moving, and covered his face with his hand, laughing.

All of this further infuriated Willie, who bellowed, "What's horses got to do with me losing my ass to you in poker every day of the week?"

Calmly, Batu explained, "Horses cannot talk. So, if you are a horseman, you have to watch them very closely, and their movements tell you how they are doing, what they need."

Now it was very quiet around the table. No one was moving their lips. They realized that Batu might be telling them something important. The wind switched, and now they were smelling the latrine. The sun was low over the stockade walls, and it was beginning to get very cold. Soon they would move inside the hovel, trying to stay warm.

Willie looked across at Batu, his head angled and his braided beard's red ribbon hanging somewhat limply today, and quietly asked, "Hmm. So, I'm a horse?"

"Precisely."

Nyam and Cheech laughed uproariously, loving every moment of this exchange.

Batu explained, "All my life, I have watched the horses for any sign whatsoever. It has been my trade, dealing with horses. It has been my life. I am, you would say, tuned in to any message that the horse will give me."

"Humans, I would say, are much like horses in this regard, only they talk too much."

Willie asked, "So when I have a good hand, I give off a message?"

"Yes, you do." Batu confirmed.

"What do I do?" Willie asked.

"Can't tell you," Batu responded. "If I tell you, I might not keep winning."

"Shit," Willie said, shaking his head, the red ribbon flying. The crew was laughing again.

"I've been watching you, too, Batu. You are playing cards very hard every day. You are almost fanatically going from game to game in the yard, winning as much as you can. Why are you pushing so hard for the money?" asked Willie.

Batu got very serious. There was no laughter now. It was very quiet at the table.

He answered, "I'm trying to save Nyam's life."

The crew stared at Batu in astonishment. Nyam was shocked, his lip was not twitching now. It trembled, looking strange on his broad face.

"Whatever do you mean?" asked Willie.

Batu answered, "There is not enough money in the deal to keep Nyam alive outside the walls."

Willie nodded at this revelation, and looked at Cheech, who was hunched over, looking at the dirt in the yard.

Willie asked, "How much more have you won?"

"Only eight hundred dollars," Batu responded, "There's not much money in the yard, and the guards won't play with me anymore."

Nyam bristled. "I have winnings, too, for the deal, and besides, once outside the wall, I can take care of myself."

"How much do you have, Nyam?" Willie grinned. Everyone knew Nyam was a poor card player.

"One hundred dollars," Nyam answered, abashed, and again everyone laughed.

Willie got serious. "I'll bankroll the deal to get Nyam out of here safely. What the hell, Batu's taking all my money anyway."

Chapter 5
The Plan Changes

Dawn the next morning brought a tremendous thunderstorm down on the prison. The lightning was very close, and sounded like ripping fabric, followed by ground-shaking explosions and the smell of ozone. Most of those present were stoic and philosophical about the breathtaking display of nature's power. "It will either kill us or it won't" was the general attitude.

Except for Willie, who hated lightning storms. At each explosion, he dipped his head like an old dog, and cursed. Flash, BANG, dip, "fuck," or flash, BANG, dip, "shit." Those around him advised that he should be praying instead of cursing. But Willie's reflexes were quicker with profanity than with prayer. Perhaps it was his upbringing.

Finally, the storm moved on, and Willie, looking somewhat washed out, laid out the bad news. "Gentlemen," he stated rather formally, "I think Nyam's deal is snake bit."

The crew looked at each other, trying to follow Willie's thinking, and Batu asked, "You think the deal with the guards will not work?"

Willie nodded his head. "If we come at them with just more money for the deal, they will know what our concern is, and it won't change their minds. Nyam will still be toast, once he gets outside the walls."

Looking each of the crew members in the eye, Willie continued, "If we up the ante, we need a very good reason. And that reason is — we need to add another person to the escape."

Batu, always very quick, asked, with a little catch in his breath, "Who goes?"

Willie responded with an unusually soft voice, looking Batu in the eyes, "Why, you go, Batu. You've been here way too long. You really need to get out of this place."

Cheech and Nyam both nodded in agreement.

Willie shrugged, almost like a Frenchman, and said, "You two, I am convinced, can watch each other's backs better than anyone. You've been doing it all your lives."

Batu was concerned. "But Willie, how will you and Cheech survive, just the two of you, in this place?"

Willie waved his arms. "Not to worry. I'm already recruiting new blood into the organization, and hopefully poor card players. I can use some relief," he laughed.

SO WILLIE LAID OUT the new plan, with all of its parts evaluated carefully by the crew. The huge Nigerian, Batu's helper with the horses, and the remaining Russian from Dansk (who was now a true believer) were given a promotion to "middle management." With a healthy stipend, they were eager new recruits.

Uno and Dos, the compromised guard contingent, and Major Bagana, the prison second-in-command, eagerly went for the new deal: Twenty-five thousand US dollars would be paid up front for Batu and Nyam to go over the wall, with papers for safe passage to Dalandzadgad. Another twenty-five thousand would be paid upon their safe arrival and induction into the Mongolian Army. It would happen within a few weeks.

It was quiet in the hovel. The new recruits were on errands, and the old crew was drinking airag, the Mongolian drink of fermented mare's milk. They were relaxed, not even playing cards. They sensed the changes about to occur in their lives. Things would never again be the same. Even though the prison was miserable, it was something they knew and had changed to their benefit. They would be stepping out into the unknown soon.

The talk around the table was informal, light and relaxed. The four men had been together a long time, and they had been through an unbelievable circus of events.

Willie looked at Batu and mentioned, in an uncharacteristically shy manner, with a quiet voice, "Batu, you have never told us how you did it; how you disappeared for twelve days then re-appeared before us almost as fit and well-fed as when you left."

Batu was touched by Willie's quiet and sincere manner. He realized that they had become good friends over their time together. It was no longer "Willie the smuggler" and his "hired bodyguards." They were now close friends and had a strong personal bond, forged by circumstances that included a daily struggle for survival.

Batu looked at his friends. "I will show you how I did the 'hat trick.'"

BATU LED THEM TO THE stables, where the officers' horses were cared for by the prisoners. Willie, Nyam and Cheech were very quiet as they approached the stables. They were finally going to learn how Batu stayed alive and well-fed under the guards' noses.

Outside the stables, it was wet and cold from the recent storms that had upset Willie, but inside the stable, it was noticeably warmer, due to the sheer body heat of the large animals. Also, it was dry. The feeding troughs had hay and some oats for the horses. These horses were the officers' pets, and they were well cared for, especially once Batu had begun working with them.

There was very little light, with lanterns spaced occasionally along the main walkway in front of the stalls. Most of the stalls were occupied by horses, but a few of them held the tack and riding gear.

Saddles were lined up on horizontal peeled logs, with the stirrups carefully folded out of harm's way. The saddles smelled of leather and saddle soap. They were in very good condition. Harnesses, bits and reins hung in another part of the stall. Posts near the ceiling kept them from touching the ground. The leather of this riding equipment was shiny from use and soft to the touch. Braided ropes also hung from pegs driven into horizontal logs spanning the tack room. These lariats were very colorful, braided with dyed leather of different colors; red, green, black, white, blue, all woven together in a rainbow of color.

Throughout the stable was the pervasive smell of horse shit, hay, oats and the odor of the animals themselves. With the pouring rain and the wind blowing outside, it was almost cozy inside the stables, except for the pounding and thudding coming from one of the stalls.

Batu led the way to the famous mare making all the noise. As they approached the stall, they saw fresh hoof marks, dents, gashes, and broken strips of planking caused by "Satan's Whore," said to be the meanest but most beautiful horse in Mongolia. She continued to kick at the stall as she turned to them, snorting and wild-eyed. The crew kept well back, giving her plenty of room. It was said that her owner, Major Bagana, took pride in her wild spirit, but talked about her much more than he rode her.

As Batu approached Satan's Whore, a strange thing happened. She looked at Batu, neighed and gnashed her teeth once, then settled down, looking over her shoulder at Batu. Then she waited, quietly. The crew looked at Batu and the horse in amazement.

Batu explained, "I had to break her so I could hide in the only place in the prison where no one would look — in Satan's Whore's stall, under the hay, between her feet."

As they watched, Batu moved along the horse's trembling side, trailing his hand along her flank, then slid in under her feet to a small depression under the hay. The horse did not move as Batu lay in the depression, pulled hay up to cover himself, and became invisible.

Amazingly, Satan's Whore started kicking again at the back of the stall, but always away from Batu. They saw how the searchers would never look in this dangerous place with the Whore's hooves flying.

Batu safely rejoined them, brushing the hay out of his hair, and they asked, "Batu, how did you do this?"

Batu replied, "I broke her in the Comanche way. These American Indians could break a horse in ten minutes. I learned of them when I studied everything to do with horses everywhere. The American Comanche Indian would smother the horse and almost take its life away, and the horse would be broken."

Then Batu continued, "I smothered her with my hand held over her nose, and almost took her life away. Then she knew, like Willie says, who's the boss. So I could hide under her and she would be careful not to harm me. It was a good hiding place." He added, "On stable cleaning days, I would hide in the loft behind the hay piles. It was good for a short time — they never looked up."

Willie shook his head in amazement and asked, "What did you eat?"

Batu smiled, "Mare's milk, two stalls down. You can milk a mare six times a day."

Then he added, "I mixed the milk with horse blood. I would open their veins with a piece of glass I found. Makes a good soup, mixed with a few oats."

The crew was doing the lip thing again. Cheech asked, "You lived on horse blood, mare's milk, and a few oats, for twelve days?"

Batu replied, "Yes, it has been in the Mongolian diet for centuries. I did not care to try the rats."

Chapter 6
Outside the Walls

After the stable visit, the crew settled in for the evening, gathering around the stove to stay warm. Much to Willie's relief the storm had passed, except for thunder and lightning flashes to the east, and it was growing colder. The barnyard smell of wet hay and horseshit was still strong, and they could hear the rats scurrying under the floor.

Willie asked, "Did it work out, with the hayfork?"

Batu answered, "Yes. We broke two tines off the fork and wrapped the ends with leather strips from the reins, then soaked them in water to make handles. Now we have two nice daggers, like large ice picks."

"We scraped them on rocks to make them even sharper; and have been figuring out ways to hide them when being searched," Nyam added.

Willie, ever the professional smuggler, now also acting as escape coach, wanted to know more. "Have you decided on the best way to conceal them? And have you practiced the hand-off moves that I mentioned?"

"Yes, to both questions, Willie," Batu responded. "The daggers are small and are easy to tie to the inside of our forearms. The daggers will not be felt if we are patted down, and we can grab them quickly."

Batu inched forward to get a little closer to the stove, then continued, "We also practiced the hand-offs many times. When one of us is searched, we can pass the dagger to the other, using our bodies to block the moves, as you showed us. I think it will work unless too many are watching us."

Willie sat back and started a story. "I remember one time in Kuala Lumpur . . . " then he paused and said, "Never mind. I think I've told that story about a hundred times."

Nyam tried to smile, gave it up with a grimace, and changed tack. "They say the transportation to Dalandzadgad is 'arranged' but I believe the only way we can get there is by horse. The roads are mired by the spring rains and when the snow melt fills the rivers it may knock out the bridges."

"Nyam is right," Batu joined in. "This happens every year in this country since we are born." Seeing some humor in the situation, he added, "In the old days, the people used low-water bridges. When the river was up, they just waited for the water levels to drop. Now the government builds nice new bridges, and every year the rivers knock them out. This is truly the land of the horse, and you must be patient."

Cheech added fuel to the fire, and as it was very cold, the crew rolled up in blankets on the floor around the stove. They all wondered what tomorrow would bring — change, for sure, but beyond that, they had only their hopes and dreams.

The night was cold and clear, with no wind whatsoever. At this altitude, in the unusually calm and cold air, sound traveled very clearly from the prison walls. The guards could be heard in animated conversation, discussing something about a shift change.

THE NEXT MORNING, NYAM and Batu were packed and ready. They had very few possessions — a blanket each, some horsemeat rolled up in a cloth, and their daggers well hidden, tied to the inside of their left forearms. Each also had money stashed in unmentionable places on their body, at Willie's insistence.

The crew sat in the hovel, waiting for a signal from the guards. Nyam and Batu were to be included in a wood foraging detail outside the prison, from which they would not return.

They were all nervous, and the conversation helped ease the tension:

"Willie, Uno yelled at you this morning. What was that about? Was he warning you?"

"Yes, he's concerned about the money being at the other end of the trek to Dalandzadgad. It's a long way."

Batu looked at Willie. "When he yelled, he said, 'Don't trip us up on this, motherfucker,' and you said back, 'I didn't know you spoke English,' and Uno said, 'Yeah, I have a brother in Queens.'"

Willie nodded. "So?"

"Willie, what is this word, 'motherfucker'?" To Batu, the word sounded disgusting, but it did roll nicely off the tongue.

Willie reacted with a big grin, stood up in front of the crew, and straightened his filthy shirt. They looked at him in resignation, knowing another "Willie speech" was coming. Willie spread his arms like he was giving a benediction and started explaining what, to him, were the facts of life.

"I can see I've neglected a big part of your education in American language, the spicy cusswords. A basic one, I think you know, is fuck-up. A fuck-up is just something we all do every day. We all make little mistakes — it's a part of living. No big deal. Now, motherfucker, you see, describes a person who is a self-serving jerk and asshole. A low-class individual, sort of one-on-one. Then there are other words for bad situations, which can affect you, like a clusterfuck. Clusterfuck describes a situation caused by people in charge that don't know what the hell they're doing. The 'cluster' part of the work relates to Lieutenant Colonels and Majors with the oak leaf insignias. Batu, a clusterfuck is what landed you in this prison. There are also SNAFU's — for Situation Normal, All Fucked Up — referring to the messy operation of many organizations, you just live with it. Now, the last situation is a shitshow. That's when everything is chaos and confusion, fed by complete incompetence."

"Now that you have names for all these messy situations," Willie continued, "Let me ask you, what kind of situation do we have here at URBAD?"

The crew answered in unison, "This is a shitshow!"

NOT A MOMENT TOO SOON, the foraging crew was assembled in the yard. There were no good-bye hugs in this place. Batu and Nyam looked at their fellow crew members one last time and headed for the yard, appearing a little overweight, with the blankets and provisions wrapped under their coats. Sergeants Uno and Dos had departed the prison earlier on "official business."

Batu and Nyam looked back at the prison as the foraging crew walked up the muddy side hill flanking the wall. Batu said, "Nyam, my friend, I hope we never see this place again. Surely it is one of the worst hellholes on earth."

Nyam nodded. "If we do see it again, maybe we can set it on fire, warm them up a bit, for a few minutes."

As they struggled through the mud, avoiding recently made deep tracks, Nyam noticed that Batu was very alert, seeming to be on guard. Nyam had seen this look before.

"What's up, Batu?" he asked.

One of the guards in charge of the detail motioned for them to shut up and keep climbing in a tighter formation, despite the terrible condition of the road. Nyam was now on the lookout for anything unusual, but he wasn't sure what. At the top of the hill, the foraging crew took a break, winded from the long climb.

Batu murmured lowly to Nyam, "As we passed out of the gate, I saw Major Bagana watching us with binoculars, really checking us out. Then it came to me. Last night when the sound carried so well, and we could hear them talking at the guard tower. Do you remember that?"

Nyam nodded.

"They weren't talking about a shift change. They were talking about a change in the plans. Uno and Dos were arguing with the Major about something he wanted them to do, or so it seemed. I am not sure."

Nyam summarized, "So there may be a change in the plan, as of last night, but nothing was said to any of us?"

Batu nodded. "Yes. We may be 'out of the loop,' as Willie says. I wonder what's in store for us?"

They walked on with the foraging crew. Despite their concerns, they felt wonderful being in the open air, free of the prison. The land and foliage smelled so clean and free of the penetrating stench of the prison, which they could still smell on their clothes. When Batu and Nyam spoke again, they had both been thinking about their situation.

Nyam started, "As Willie said, there are some safeguards in place to protect us from the guards' treachery."

Batu nodded in agreement. "Yes, the payment by Willie's runner when we arrive in Dalandzadgad, at the arranged location. So, if the runner is not intercepted, we should be safe until then."

Batu looked around. It was almost time to go to work. He said, "Then, there is the exchange, the money for the enlistment papers. You heard Willie say it many times: 'the exchange is the most dangerous part of the deal.' He said that the exchanges were always scary. It is too easy to just eliminate the other side instead of making the trade; then you have all the goodies."

The guards motioned them forward again, and they started gathering wood to load on the horse-driven sled. The fresh cut wood smelled good in the clean untainted air. Batu and Nyam could not help but feel giddy. They smiled as they tossed the logs onto the pile.

AT MID-MORNING, UNO and Dos arrived in an ancient truck, so old and battered that its make was undecipherable. But the engine sounded good, and the tires were big. The truck was a "mudder" for the treacherous roads. It seated two in the cab, with an open hatchway aft to a flatbed with a canvas top, and bench seats along the sides of the bed.

As the truck slipped and slid up the muddy road, Batu and Nyam scrambled into the back of the old truck. They noticed that the other guards acted as if it was normal for two prisoners of their wood-foraging crew to leap aboard a passing truck. Obviously, everything was going as planned. Batu and Nyam moved up and sat on the bench seats behind the cab.

In the passenger seat was Uno, Sergeant Tugso Erdene, a large, swarthy, bald man with large brown telegraphic eyes, a long gunfighter-type mustache and a long hook nose. Batu, looking at Uno's expressive eyes, thought, *"It sure was easy to play poker with this guy."* The second sergeant, Dos, named Rentsen Dorvaa, had a look-alike, large, drooping mustache, but there the similarity ended. He was a smaller man, with abundant bushy black hair, and black eyes that revealed nothing.

Dos was skillfully driving the truck, seeming to shift at just the right moment to keep them moving through the mud. Both Uno and Dos were wearing vests with 7.62-millimeter Tokarev TT-33 pistols in a sewn-in pouch under their left arm, ready for quick access. Nyam, ever the professional soldier, raised his eyebrows slightly as he admired their gear. There was an air of tension about the sergeants, a wary alertness that was palpable.

Dos cut right to the chase. "We have heard much about the exploits of you two, and we will not hesitate to kill you both if you make any threatening moves whatsoever."

Uno looked over at his cohort, surprised a little by his outburst, and said, "Yes, we will show no mercy, we will shoot you down like dogs."

Quickly, Batu responded, "Sirs, we have much to gain by making this agreement work. I can assure you that the money will be in Dalandzadgad. Willie Barron has never failed us."

Then, trying to diffuse the tense situation with an attempt at humor, Batu asked, smiling, "Sergeant Dos, Sergeant Uno, will we be riding this fine vehicle all the way to Dalandzadgad?"

Uno twitched his large mustache and answered curtly, "Yes, if the poor roads and high rivers permit. There is fuel stashed along the route." Then Dos accelerated the old truck, mud started flying, and they were on their way to Dalandzadgad.

BACK AT THE PRISON, Willie "the Goat" Barron laid in his bunk and looked at the ceiling. He had been very quiet lately, and Cheech stayed near him like a shadow, to protect him and perhaps, to talk.

Cheech, uncharacteristically speaking more since Batu and Nyam had left, asked, "Willie, are you worried about Batu and Nyam?"

Willie rolled over on his side to face Cheech, looked past him at the empty doorway, and answered, "Yeah, Cheech, I'm worried about them on the road, and about what might happen to them when they get to Dalandzadgad, at the exchange, money for papers." He added, "My best runner is on that job. I'm sure the money will be there. I think."

Willie dropped a leg out of the bunk and swung his foot back and forth restlessly. Cheech noticed that his homemade socks had holes in them, and his feet were red from the cold.

Cheech started sharpening Batu's knife again. He looked up and asked an unanswerable question, "I wonder if we'll ever see Batu and Nyam again?"

Willie looked at the floor and shrugged.

Chapter 7
Threats

On the mountain road, the old truck clattered past snowbanks and cedar trees, with mud building up under the wheel wells.

Near a large ravine, Uno suddenly barked, "Okay. Turn off here. Park near that large tree by the ravine."

Dos pulled the truck over and killed the engine. Then Uno was out of the truck and beside the tailgate, pistol in hand. Batu and Nyam tensed. Why were they stopping?

"Out, now, quick," Uno shouted, waving his gun. "Get over by the ravine, face out, backs to us! — Move! Be quick!"

Nyam and Batu climbed slowly out the back of the truck, trying to assess the situation, unsure of Uno's intent. Batu was thinking, *"I may need to put the dagger in him, but the other one is covering us."* Then he noticed, *"The weapon is not cocked, he has not worked the slide."*

Nyam and Batu stood stiffly by the ravine's edge, sweating in the cold. As they looked out at the beautiful mountains, they wondered if this was where they would die. Nyam thought of Onor, and Batu had a strong urge to urinate.

Then Uno said, "Hold your arms up! Let Rentsen search you."

As Rentsen (Dos) went to search Batu, Nyam discreetely loosened the spike on his arm, ready to strike. Dos roughly patted down Batu, but didn't find anything.

Then, patting Nyam down, Dos exclaimed, "What is this?! Do you have a weapon?" Then, relaxing, he answered his own question, "Ah, it is meat. We will have an early lunch."

Chapter 8
Treachery

Following the search, they were back on the road again with changes in the seating arrangement. Nyam, the big one, was ordered to sit in the right front seat. Uno sat behind Dos on the bench seat in back, so he could watch both Nyam and Batu, who was across from him on the other bench seat, just behind Nyam.

It was a good position for Uno, as he could quickly pull and fire at both of them with just a small arc of the Tokarev. Smiling, Uno congratulated himself on his defense tactics. The only problem was that he was now sitting on the hard bench seat in back, instead of the relatively soft seat up front.

Batu, ever curious, started asking questions about the trip, watching Uno's expressive eyes for signs of treachery.

"Sergeant Erdene, how long do you think it will take to get to Dalandzadgad?"

Uno (Erdene) responded knowledgeably, "The trip is about eighteen hundred kilometers. If we can average twenty-five kilometers an hour, or about two hundred kilometers a day on these roads, the driving time should be about nine days. When you add in the stops for food, fuel and breaks, it should take about twelve days total."

Impressed, Batu offered, "That's a long way. We can help with the driving, if you would trust us that much."

After giving Batu a long, slow look, Uno said, "We will see."

Nyam turned and joined in, "Sir, you have the route plotted?"

Uno responded as though the answer was obvious, "Of course. We will travel along the foothills of the Altai Mountains. The road will take us to the village of Dzereg, about three hundred kilometers, then another three hundred kilometers to the town of Altai."

Uno peered at the canvas roof, seeing the route in his mind. "From Altai, it is another nine hundred kilometers to Dalandzadgad, but unfortunately the good road turns northeast towards Ulan Bator. So, from Altai, we have to take much lesser roads for the last nine hundred kilometers." Then he added, "Those lesser roads are going to be a challenge."

Nyam and Batu looked at each other. It was going to be quite a journey. They shook their heads.

Dos spoke up, "You can see that we are earning our money."

The ancient truck continued along the muddy, rutted road that cut across a steep side hill, with high banks on one side and a breathtaking drop into a deep canyon on the other side. There were no guard rails, nothing to keep them from tumbling over the edge to oblivion with a careless move. It took their breath away — so much height, a second-by-second potential for immediate disaster. No one talked. The strain on their nerves was constant and fatiguing.

Batu noticed that Uno was terrified of the heights. His eyes were large, his breath was coming in short gasps, and his hands were trembling. It was good that Dos was driving.

As the truck skidded from side to side along the precipice, to escape the numbing fear of suddenly going over the side, Batu forced himself to think of other things. What was his future? What did he really want? He considered this, and realized his wants were simple. He wanted his friends to be safe, away from the seemingly endless day-to-day struggle to stay alive. Also, he wanted to be someplace warm. He was tired of the cold all of the time. It seemed like he had been in the cold most of his life. He thought maybe the theory that Hell was cold instead of hot might be true. And his last wish, or want, was to be with horses. He loved horses. Also, he thought with a smile, maybe Onor has a sister.

BY NIGHTFALL, THEY had traveled only about a hundred kilometers, but thankfully, were off of the side hill on more level ground. They nosed the old truck into a grove of aspen trees and had a dinner of coarse brown bread and horsemeat. They were exhausted from the ordeal of cliff-edge driving on a muddy, slick road. The recent "escapees," in spite of their exhaustion, were having a good time.

"Delicious bread," Batu exclaimed as he gnawed on the hard coarse bread. It was new to him and Nyam. So much better than prison food.

Their next surprise, "Mountain sleeping bags with zippers?"

Nyam tried to smile, causing the sergeants to flinch. Batu and Nyam climbed into the sleeping bags that had been stored under the seats; and were asleep in minutes in the comparative luxury. The grizzled sergeants just looked at each other and shook their heads, as they climbed into their bags. There was room to sleep in the truck, two on the aft seats and two on the truck bed. The guards slept with their guns at the ready.

The next two days were uneventful. The roads improved and they made better time. Batu noticed that the two guards were more nervous and stressed than would seem normal. They seemed worried and jumpy. Batu tried to draw them out with conversation, sometimes difficult over the clatter of the old truck's diesel engine.

"Will there be roadblocks ahead?" Batu asked. He knew the army liked to check papers with impromptu roadblocks.

Both Uno and Dos looked startled by the question, but recovered quickly and Uno responded, "Yes, there will be roadblocks, but we have the proper paperwork. Don't worry."

Batu looked at Nyam, who turned in the seat and was observing the sergeants curiously. Nyam had caught it, and Batu had sensed it as well. There would be trouble for them at a roadblock. Their instincts, honed by years of day-to-day survival in the prison, told them of the trouble to come. Batu and Nyam looked at each other, and Batu raised an eyebrow as if to say, "what's next?"

THEY ENTERED THE VILLAGE of Dzereg on the morning of the third day. The village was small, with narrow streets and sod buildings, interspersed occasionally with yurts, the traditional round shelters that were well engineered to withstand the harshest of Mongolian winters. The streets were muddy, with ditches down the middle to accommodate the snowmelt drainage. The smell of wood smoke permeated the air. The travelers topped off all the tanks with diesel, then did some provisioning, including more presentable clothes for Nyam and Batu, and a treat — a meal in a restaurant, and a bath house visit.

Nyam and Batu exited the bath house feeling like new men. They were clean, with new clothes, and daggers still concealed, as they had not been watched closely. They had the money for these luxuries due to Willie's insistence on them carrying a stash, always. The sergeants, when searching them, had been looking for weapons, not concealed money. They seemed unconcerned that their prisoners were able to pay their way, and were gleeful that they got to share in the benefits. The guards seemed to relax as they spent time with their prisoners.

As they approached the truck, Uno said, "Another three hundred kilometers to Altai, then the roads become worse. Nyam, why don't you take a turn at the wheel? Let's see how well you drive."

Nyam tried to smile. "My field is reconnaissance. I can drive anything."

The drive to Altai was uneventful. The high-desert road was passable, and the four Mongolians discussed food, horses, women and professions, in random order.

Uno spoke of his trade, "I am a cobbler, and I love the work." He twitched his great mustache, and his expressive eyes grew dreamy. "I had a great cobbler shop, with lasts that would fit any foot," he boasted, and glanced at Nyam's huge feet. "With my share of the money, I'm going to open another cobbler shop in my hometown, when I get out of the army."

"I was told," he went on, "that I would make boots in the army." He sniffed and shook his head, "Instead, I man a gun on the wall at URBAD. I hate that job."

The conversation shifted to horse races, a favorite pastime of most Mongolians. Dos, who was a wrangler by trade, had strong opinions about racehorses.

"I believe," he said, "that the grays have the best stamina for the thirty-kilometer cross-country races, and they are beautiful animals, with their roman noses and beer bellies. The grays have real character."

Batu nodded earnestly. He loved to talk of horses, especially racehorses. "The grays," Batu ventured, "have the best feet for the rough terrain. But I've won the most on brown horses with black manes."

Next, Dos spoke of a legendary dancer he had known by the name Kokoma. "She was very beautiful, and a magnificent dancer. I was with her many times — until my money was gone." There was laughter in the truck. Then Dos smiled, with a faraway look in his eyes, and said, "She was a beautiful creature." More laughter.

DOS RESUMED DRIVING. Batu looked at Nyam, whose eyes were scanning the ridges and ravines, ever cautious. As the truck clattered down the road toward Altai, Uno pulled out a map and some notes.

Looking at them, he announced, "We will make a small detour about sixty-five kilometers from Altai. We will turn off to Sharga, where we will meet two men, to help see us the rest of the way."

Batu was immediately cautious, asking, "These men are needed to help us?"

"They will have the details of the final meeting and the money exchange. It's a timed thing. Your drug smuggler's courier is to meet us with the other half of the money at Bulgan, the small village outside Dalanzadgad."

"Why Sharga?" asked Nyam, also suspicious of the plan.

"It's a small village, and isolated," Uno answered, "located at a dead-end road. It's a good place for a meeting."

"These new guys," Dos added, "will know the details of the trade and timing — when your courier will arrive."

Batu dipped his head and looked at his feet. He was thinking of the timing and the distance. How could the new guys know the timing of their arrival outside Dalandzadgad when they still had nine hundred kilometers to go, across a stretch of the Gobi Desert? It was simply too early to tell when they would get there for the exchange. So why meet now, in this remote village off the main road?

Batu looked at Nyam, who was not driving at the time, and shook his head ever so slightly. He saw that Nyam got the message, as Nyam casually rested his right hand on his left forearm, where the dagger lay concealed.

The route to Sharga required them to stay on the main road to Altai, crossing over a deep ravine by a bridge, then cutting back to the southwest along the ravine for twenty-five kilometers to the small village. Uno was visibly nervous again as they traveled along the ravine. Sharga was truly an out-of-the-way place, where most anything could happen unnoticed. The ride had grown very quiet, with little being said in the truck. Each had their own thoughts; Batu and Nyam's being mainly of survival.

As they entered the village, they saw, off to the right by an old barn, a man waving them into the barn entrance.

Batu asked, "These are the friends of yours?"

Uno responded, "I don't know them, but they have red armbands on, the signal."

Batu noticed that the mud-splattered car by the barn wall had been there for some time. They had been waiting. The two men smiled and waved them inside the barn door.

"Come on in and have some tea," one of them said, "my name is Dorgon, you may have noticed there's a town named after me," and he smiled again.

He was of medium build, needed a shave, was somewhat swarthy looking and did not look like he normally smiled so much.

Batu noticed right away that the ever-smiling Dorgon had a machine pistol, one of those Chinese jobs, in a shoulder rig under his left arm. Also, — Batu could hardly believe it — the machine pistol was cocked with the safety off.

Smiley's partner, a huge man wearing a shaggy overcoat open in front, moved up closer and also waved them in, smiling but saying nothing.

Nyam climbed off the truck and moved close to the big man.

He said, "I sure could use some tea. It was a long trip."

Batu moved left and forward, near Smiley's right. Uno and Dos approached Dorgon (Smiley) and his big friend to shake hands with their co-conspirators. Dorgon suddenly raised his machine pistol and swung it left to right on full automatic, making a chattering, scything sound as the muzzle came up. Four rounds caught Dos across the chest, driving him back into the hay and soft mud of the barn. Blood pumped from the holes in his chest, and he made a sucking sound as he lay on his back.

The chattering machine pistol barely missed Uno because the automatic weapon had kicked up and was blowing holes in the loft at the top of the barn. Uno fell to his knees in shock, expecting Smiley to correct his aim. Instead, he saw Smiley stand there for a moment, with a look of surprise on his face, then he toppled backward with a dagger sticking out of his chest. He was sputtering and in obvious pain.

Uno looked around for the big stranger, and found him laid out in a stall with his head at an unnatural angle. Nyam had broken the big man's neck.

As Smiley lay dying with the dagger in his chest, Batu picked up the machine pistol and collected an extra clip from the dying man's belt, as he calmly gave instructions on firing such a gun.

"When you fire this beast on full-automatic," Batu told the dying man, "The recoil pulls the barrel way up. It's best to fire short bursts at the target."

Then Batu knelt by the man and asked, "Who are you working for? Are you working for the Major with the binoculars?"

Smiley gurgled, his feet bouncing as his body convulsed, and he died. Batu tried to remove the dagger from Smiley's chest. It was stuck fast; it must have hit his backbone. Batu pulled again and again. Finally, the dagger popped free, and with it, a fountain of blood spurted up into Batu's face. He stepped back and wiped at his face with his hand, but only smeared it.

Batu looked up at Nyam and asked, "You ever see anything like this before?"

Nyam gave Batu a funny look, and said. "No, Batu, nothing like this, ever."

Nyam checked the perimeter, and Batu went to make Dos comfortable, but it was all over for him. He was dying, but muttered one word, then lay still, looking out at the world with unseeing eyes.

Nyam asked Batu, "What did he say?"

"He said 'Kokoma.'"

Uno had crawled up into a corner of the stall, in shock. He had not even drawn his weapon. It had happened so fast, and now his friend, Sergeant Dorvaa, was dead.

He muttered to Batu, "I can't believe this happened, and Rentsen is dead. So quick." And he hugged himself and rocked back and forth.

Batu pointed out the obvious. "They wanted to kill the two of you, not Nyam and me." He knelt beside Uno and said, "More money at the payout for them, I guess. Who are they, anyway?"

There was no response.

Batu bent over, stared into Uno's eyes and asked forcefully, "Do you know them?"

Uno shook his head and said nothing.

Nyam reconned the area thoroughly. No one had heard; no one was coming. The site had been well selected. Batu and Nyam moved quickly, now in charge. Batu carried Dos' Tokarev, and Nyam held the machine pistol with two clips. After a quick exchange of glances, Batu and Nyam let Uno keep his pistol and treated him respectfully, but he was still in shock at this totally unexpected event. Batu and Nyam seemed to know what to do, so Uno did not argue with their benevolent takeover.

NOT KNOWING WHAT THEY were up against, they decided not to return to the main road. Checking Uno's map, they decided to cut across-country toward two small villages, Halion and Tseel, to procure horses for a cross-country trek to Bulgan, outside Dalandzadgad, where supposedly, the exchange was still to take place. They reasoned that Willie's man and the money would show up there.

Moving quickly, they searched the killers' bodies for information, but found none. They removed the giant stranger's boots, which fit Nyam perfectly. The car, an obscure Chinese model with a white swan hood ornament, held a map and a fine pair of German-made binoculars.

Nyam handed the binoculars to Uno, and as they loaded the bodies into the car, said, "You will need to drive this car until we can find a place to dump it."

Uno did not like the idea of his "prisoners," Batu and Nyam, driving off in the truck, with him following in a car full of bodies. What if they just left and kept on going?

Uno made a counter suggestion, "Batu should drive the car."

Nyam looked at Uno, almost imploringly, and said, "YOU should drive the car, not Batu. You don't even want to know why."

They looked at each other, at an impasse. It was a test of faith. Uno thought about it, and realized they could kill him any time, anyway.

He shrugged, shook his head and said, "Okay, I'll drive the car."

They tossed the killers in the back seat and, almost reverently, sat the dead Dos in the front seat for his last ride. Just before nightfall, they found a steep, flooded ravine and rolled the white swan and its passengers to their final resting place, after a short prayer for Rentsen Dorvaa.

Chapter 9
On the Run, Horse Trading

Nyam drove along the narrow road, his eyes scanning for any type of pursuit. In the back, Batu tilted a canteen of water over his face to wash off the blood, then turned his coat inside out to hide the gore. Uno was recovering fast now, sitting in the front passenger seat.

"I don't know who those men were," Uno said, frowning. "I had never seen them before." Then Uno looked directly into Batu's eyes and said, "Major Bagana, the one with the binoculars, gave me the instructions about the turn off just before we left URBAD." Then Uno looked at Nyam, and added, "The Major must have set us up to be eliminated."

Batu reasoned, "I think you're right. Their car had seating for only four. And it makes no sense to kill Nyam and me now, before the money is delivered. The money is to be given only upon our safe arrival."

Uno summed it up, shaking his head sadly, "Betrayal and murder, for profit."

As the old truck slipped and slid along the trail, Batu thought of what they needed: food, shelter, rest, and horses. They were worn out from the encounter at the barn and the necessity of dumping three human beings in a ravine like so much garbage. It was all bad karma, and they needed help.

Not an hour later, as the truck rattled around a bend and over a small rise, they saw below them a large corral of horses, near an old house and barn. There were two old trucks out back, much like the one they were driving.

Batu looked at the scene in disbelief. It looked like an answer to his prayers. If only he could make what he had in mind come to pass.

THE TRIO DROVE THEIR truck into the driveway of the old house, and out of courtesy, waited to be recognized. Batu noticed the house was in ill repair, and one of the trucks had a wheel missing. Engine parts lay on the hood.

The front door opened, and a wizened old man stepped boldly out on the front porch, peering at them as he said, "Eh?"

Uno started with a well-planned dialog, "Hello, Grandfather. We have been traveling a long way and would like to rest here for a bit, if we may."

The old man tilted forward, ambled up to the truck, looked them over, gave them a toothless grin, saying, "You drink airag?"

As Uno responded, "Yes, Grandfather, we do!" everyone in the truck felt a sense of relief. Maybe their prayers had been answered.

They drank airag well into the night, gathered around a red-hot stove. Stew and black bread were served, and Grandfather Khentii proved to be an excellent host and storyteller. Uno brought the sleeping bags in, and they slept, warm at last, draped around the big stove.

The next morning, rested and refreshed, the negotiations began.

Batu, as the recognized horse expert, opened. "Grandfather, we would like to acquire six horses and three saddles, tack, and pack frames for three."

"Well, boy," Khentii responded, "You've come to the right place. I'm a horse trader."

Batu, feeling on good ground, offered, "We are willing to pay one thousand, five hundred Tughrik for the horses and tack."

Immediately, Khentii shook his head no. "You will have to pay much more; much, much more. These are very good horses."

Batu responded in a very surprised voice, "Grandfather, with all due respect, your horses are old, underfed, and some of them look sick."

Khentii was taken aback, and offended. "You are but a puppy, Batu, and the Mongol knowledge of horses must have been passed down to your little sister."

As these exchanges took place, Nyam and Uno took refuge in the shade of the front porch, their feet up, drinking airag and watching the show. Uno, the cobbler, looked worried.

He asked Nyam, "Do you think this trade will work out?"

Nyam smiled and said, "This is normal for a horse trade. It may take a while, but you can be assured that Batu is very good at this."

By evening, the trade still had not been resolved, and negotiations were suspended for another evening of food, airag, and storytelling.

As they prepared their bedrolls that night, Nyam asked Batu, "How is the trade going?"

"You know these trades sometimes take a while," Batu smiled. "He gave us a tell. I will move on it in the morning."

Uno, curious, asked, "What kind of tell?"

"He likes the truck. I saw his eyebrow raise when he looked at it, as he stepped off the porch. And he keeps looking that way," Batu responded.

"What if it was just a twitch?" Uno asked.

"If it was just a twitch, we may all be walking," Batu laughed.

BATU, NYAM AND UNO prepared to depart the next morning with six fine horses, three saddled and three on leads with their provisions on pack frames. Grandfather Khentii, since he got a good price for the horses, and a truck as well, had made the mistake of allowing Batu his pick of the horses in the large corral.

"You took the very best," Khentii whined as Batu selected the stock.

Batu responded, good naturedly, in the vein of all horse traders, "You are an old bandit, Grandfather, and you know you skinned us on this trade."

Khentii cackled with pleasure, enjoying the whole affair, and said philosophically, "Anybody that trades is going to get skinned occasionally," and he waved goodbye, saying, "Hope to see you boys again sometime."

The trio chuckled and shook their heads as they thought about Khentii, such a colorful character. They rode east toward Bulgan and Dalanzadgad, some eight hundred kilometers distant. They were rested, well fed, and on good horses, so they made good time on the well-marked cross-country trails, following Nyam, a natural trail blazer.

As they walked the horses to cool them down, in preparation to shifting to riding the pack horses, Batu moved near Uno in a friendly manner. Batu wanted to know more about the planned exchange, at the small village of Bulgan.

He asked, "Sergeant Erdene, do you know the details of the place where we'll make the exchange?"

"Your smuggler friend, Willie Barron, set up the money transfer," said Uno. "He is very clever."

"What do you mean?" Batu asked, although he thought he knew some of what Uno was going to say. Willie had told him of the transfer.

Uno continued, "By going up a single lane road that dead ends into Bulgan, the runner will recognize you from Willie's description, and will bring the money to you on the way to the village." Uno nodded as he added, "You then go to the meeting, and give the money to the major in exchange for the Army enlistment papers. I understand that Army officials in Dalanzadgad have been bribed to make the enlistment process move smoothly."

Batu nodded. Willie had told him much the same.

Then Uno surprised him with his insight. "What troubles me, Batu, is the last-minute note from Major Bagana, ordering the detour where we were machine gunned. This makes me realize that I am very expendable in the minds of whoever is in charge."

Uno hunched his shoulders, as if expecting bullets, and said, "I think I may be riding to my death."

With a wry smile, Batu noted, "Don't worry, Tugso. In the Major's mind, you are already dead."

Chapter 10
The Swinging Bridge

The trio rode hard for the next five days, mindful that they were moving slower than planned, as they were on horseback, but comfortable with the custom in that when you travel in Mongolia, timelines were fluid. It seemed that you were always late in this country.

The trail followed along the slopes of the Altai Mountains, and the vegetation was growing sparse as they neared the Gobi Desert. The terrain was very rough. Discussions were sporadic.

Uno observed that Nyam and Batu were tremendous horsemen, seeming to glide over the rock and brush with ease. He knew he was holding them back, and he knew that they knew enough about the exchange that they didn't need him anymore. He expected that they would kill him soon. He cursed his luck, dealing with two factions, neither of which needed him alive. Were it not for the money, he would run for it. But with his share of the money, Uno would start his cobbler shop. He had daydreamed of the exact layout that his shop would have, where the leather would be stored, how the lasts would line up, the boxes of brads and tacks, the smell of the polishes and new leather. He would have the best sewing machine money could buy. Uno could see it all in his mind's eye — it had been his dream for years.

One evening, when they were relaxed by the campfire, Uno told Batu and Nyam of his dream, and even though they seemed interested, he felt foolish for telling it. He did not know why.

The spring-like weather was warmer, as they headed southeast toward the great desert. flowers were in bloom and beautiful little gray birds with black topknots and a trace of red in their wings, flew back and forth before them, leading them away from their nests. Uno found all this very beautiful, because he felt that his days were surely numbered. He would die soon.

ON THEIR FIFTH DAY on horseback, they came to a cable suspension bridge across the huge ravine with the Orog river rushing and tumbling two-hundred meters below. It was an awesome spectacle, and they camped at the bridge head and looked at the hundred-meter cable bridge spanning the ravine before them. It made their stomachs churn.

The suspension bridge was old and scary looking. The main cables at the bridgehead were frayed; and appeared to be merely wedged between rocks to hold the entire structure. The cables were worn, green, and mostly rusty, with broken strands unraveling to form small bird-nest-looking knots at the cable terminals.

The walkway across the bridge looked like a snaggle-tooth piano, with some missing, broken, or rotten-looking boards. To Batu, the bridge looked like it had been hurriedly cobbled together in another era and left abandoned for no intended further use.

Batu took a few cautious steps out on the bridge and looked over the suspension cable at the roaring river in the canyon far below. It took his breath away. The river was all white water careening between the steep walls and tumbling over huge boulders, sending spray high into the air. The power of the river was truly spectacular. As Batu gaped straight down at the raging river, he noticed a sign on a ledge ten meters below him. It had fallen off the bridge, and it said, "No Horses." He hoped Uno would not see it.

They built a small fire, broke out their provisions, and gave some water and a touch of oats to the horses. Sleeping bags were rolled out and they tried to relax.

Batu made clear his intentions. "We have to cross that bridge. There is no other way, as you can see."

Uno responded, "I don't like heights. I can hardly breathe when I'm up high."

"I know. I saw you having difficulties on the side hills in the truck," said Batu.

Uno, embarrassed, nodded. "Yes. It is very difficult for me."

Nyam adjusted himself by the fire, and took another bite of Grandfather's coarse, hard, black bread. He thought it was delicious.

Nyam said, "I will go across first. The bridge is only one meter wide, so there will be no turning back with the horses. I have done this type of bridge before. We should go early, because the wind will be calmer, and take two horses each." He laid back on the sleeping bag, as if the matter was settled, and it was not a big thing.

Batu looked at Uno. "I will go second. By the time Nyam and I are across, with four horses, you will see how easily it can be done." And then Batu smiled a disarming smile that Uno had not seen before.

The camp was peaceful that night, as all their camps had been along the way, for this was a very remote area. Batu and Nyam were asleep almost instantly. They really liked the warm mountain sleeping bags. Uno, who had the watch, worried about the bridge. He was terrified of it. He lay there, listening to the horses munch on the short bushes and thought of happier days, when he was a cobbler.

BATU WAS UP BEFORE dawn the next morning, chewing on black bread and tending the horses, combing them and feeding them bits of bush he had gathered.

"They are not getting enough water," Batu said. "The extra water we packed is almost gone."

Nyam returned. He had been checking out the bridge. "I walked it, there are some bad boards, but the support cables at the bridgehead look good."

Uno swallowed hard and shook his head.

Nyam started giving instructions, as if he had done this tour every day. "We will go across one at a time, each with two horses on long leads." He looked at Uno appraisingly. "Move steadily, but if the horses step too much together, the bridge will start swinging. If this happens, you must stop, let the bridge settle, then start again."

Batu added for Uno's benefit, "Too much synchronized rhythm will make a suspension bridge swing. You know of this?"

Uno shook his head, no. Shit. A moving bridge with bad boards, two-hundred meters above a raging river. *"I do not feel well,"* he thought. He had not slept much that night.

They started while the weather was calm. Nyam moved slowly and steadily across the bridge, talking to the horses to calm them. Then Nyam's second horse stepped on a board that cracked under its weight, spooking the horse. It stopped and started neighing, looking at the river below with the whites of his eyes showing. Nyam could not go back. He stood there, waiting. Batu moved forward alone on the bridge, squeezed beside Nyam's packhorse, and started to calm the animal, talking to it. He smoothly blindfolded the horse with the torn-off sleeves of his shirt. The horse calmed, and Batu, patting the horse, moved back to the bridgehead.

Uno was amazed at Batu's forethought. He had taken off his coat and shirt, and cut the shirtsleeves for the blindfold, as Nyam had started across. Batu had anticipated the problem.

As Batu called, "Go, Nyam," Nyam started again, crossing the bridge very slowly.

Uno was holding his breath, and saying "Shit, shit, shit," — words he had learned at the prison walls.

Nyam made it across the bridge without further incident, tethered the horses, and started scouting the far rim immediately. They did not want any surprises. Batu started preparing his horses to go across next. Although it was never said, Batu went next in case Uno froze up and could not make it, leaving Batu stranded.

As Batu worked, he started questioning Uno. "Sergeant, where are you from?"

Uno answered, knowing that Batu was trying to calm him, "I'm from the village of Hanh, in far northern Mongolia, just south of the Irkut River, which is just across the Russian border. It is in a beautiful valley, by a lake. I made boots for Russians as well as Mongols." Uno knew he was talking too much at this time, but he was nervous.

Batu smiled as he started leading his horses to the bridge, and asked, "You will have your cobbler shop there, someday?"

"Yes. My enlistment is up soon, and that's my hope."

Then Batu turned and looked at Uno, and said, "When I reach the other side, start moving across, slowly and steadily. Talk to the horses to calm them. If the horses get too excited, I will come with the blindfold. You just hold the horses steady, okay?"

Uno nodded. His mouth was very dry.

Batu started across, then stopped, turned back, and said to Uno, "I noticed that you don't talk to your horses much. I wish you talked to them more."

Uno looked at Batu, shook his head, and said, "Fuck! Now you tell me!"

Batu threw his head back and laughed from deep inside, and Uno, to his surprise, laughed also. *"What is this,"* Uno thought, *"gallows humor?"* But he did feel a little better.

Batu moved smoothly across the suspension bridge, and, as he had advised, talked to his horses. But about one third of the way across, the bridge started swinging, as the horses were too much in step. Batu had to stop. The horses did not like the swinging, and they did not like to stop. They started getting skittish, and Batu calmed them, talking soothingly. Then Batu moved forward again, making it another third of the way across, before the swinging started again. As Batu stopped the horses once more, he realized that the wind was picking up, blowing up the canyon, adding to the swaying movement. *"Oh my,"* Batu thought, *"This is not going to go well for Uno."* Batu talked to the horses and pushed the lead horse to the center of the narrow bridge. Then he was on the move again, and they made it across. Batu exhaled a sigh of relief, realizing that he did not like heights, either.

Nyam was waiting. He said, "The wind is coming up, fast."

Batu nodded, looked back across the bridge, and saw that Uno was already on his way across, leading the horses. Even from a distance, Uno's face looked white.

"Oh my," Batu voiced again, "This doesn't look good for Uno."

They noticed that Uno, in his nervousness, was moving too fast, and the horses were shaking their heads back and forth, spooked by the bridge. Then the bridge started swinging.

As Batu and Nyam watched helplessly, the horses panicked and began running across the bridge, right over Uno, trampling him and knocking him over the side between the cables. Then, as they ran and the bridge swung, both horses got off-center. The bridge tilted severely, breaking an upper cable and dumping the animals over the side. The horses screamed all the way down to the river. It was a horrifying sound that would haunt them for years. The horses hit with a large splash, and one horse grew silent, but the other continued to scream and scream, as the river took it all the way around the bend.

Even as it was still swinging, Batu ran pell-mell onto the bridge. He had seen Uno go off the bridge, but had not seen him fall. As he ran, Batu saw a boot stuck in a vee of the cable, and his heart sank. That was all that was left of Uno. Batu slowed down and shook his head sadly — but then noticed that Uno was still hanging by his boot from the bridge.

Batu screamed, "Nyam, get a line!" as he ran to Uno and dove for the occupied boot, grabbing Uno's leg by his britches with one hand, and holding the cable with the other. Uno's booted foot was wedged in a cable junction, but he was slowly slipping out of the boot. Batu knew he could not hold on for long, and was yelling for Nyam.

As Uno's foot slid out of the boot, Batu could not hold him, and Uno fell, just as Nyam's line looped around his neck and one arm. Uno continued to fall, pulling Batu against a cable block and breaking his nose. Then Uno swung free of Batu's grasp, head down, until he hit the end of Nyam's line and jerked around. Although lucky that his neck was not broken, Uno started to choke to death. Nyam pulled the choking Uno back up to the bridge, with Batu helping, his broken nose bleeding on Nyam's line. Uno's face was very red, and as they hoisted him over the lower rail, he didn't appear to be breathing any longer.

"Goddammit," Nyam swore. "We saved him, then we killed him."

As they laid Uno gently out on the swinging bridge and freed the line from around his ravaged neck, they noticed he was struggling to breathe. Quickly, Nyam flipped Uno onto his stomach and held him steady on the swaying bridge, for now the wind was really blowing. Batu pounded Uno's back, heavy blows, to get him breathing better, and suddenly Uno vomited, then curled up into a fetal position. He was alive.

To get off the treacherous bridge, still swinging in the wind, Batu and Nyam had to edge sideways over the broken boards, holding the remaining upper cable with one hand, with Uno held between them. Uno was only partially conscious and was not much help.

They finally made the bridge head, and exhausted, laid Uno in the dirt while they caught their breath. Uno started regaining consciousness. Still terrified, he made a keening sound and started pushing with his heels in the dirt, scraping along backwards on his shoulder blades.

Batu, trying to calm Uno, said to Nyam, "Well, hell, are we going to have to sit on him now? On top of everything else?"

Nyam snickered and replied, "Well, I guess we could drive a stake in him."

After finally getting Uno calmed down and sleeping, Batu and Nyam foraged and found an excellent concealed campsite, not far from a stream where they could water the horses. They used boughs and canvas to fashion a shelter; and prepared some food from the remaining provisions.

Uno drifted in and out of consciousness as he lay on saddle blankets under the shelter. He was battered and bruised from the trampling, his neck was raw and swollen, and his leg had long striated bruises where he had hung from the bridge. Batu used an odorous grease from the pack frames on Uno's neck, and although it stank, it seemed to help.

On the afternoon of the second day of encampment, Uno woke enough to talk in a scratchy voice. He could barely be heard, and Batu had to lean close to hear what he had to say.

Batu laughed, and Nyam, trying to smile, asked, "What?"

Batu repeated Uno's message. "He said, after that bridge, he's not even going to use high bar stools."

THUS, THE RECOVERY began, and Uno was amazed at the patience and respect shown by Batu and Nyam towards a prison guard who had been transporting them for profit. Although he had seen them kill with chilling efficiency, he realized that they had character, a code of honor, and a sense of propriety that he had seldom seen. He no longer feared they would kill him. After all, they had risked their lives to save him.

Batu, looking like a raccoon with his broken nose and two black eyes, handed Uno a sandal he had fashioned of coiled stitched rope and woven horsehair, saying "Can't have a barefoot cobbler with only one boot." He harassed him further, "For a man who's been trampled, stretched, hung and pounded on, you don't look so bad."

Nyam laughed and added, "Almost better than Batu. I will practice my roping when I have the time. I was aiming for your shoulders!"

Uno croaked in his scratchy voice, "I'm sorry about the horses, My god, that was awful. I can still hear them screaming."

Batu, who loved horses, shook his head sadly in agreement.

The next morning, Uno tested his mobility. He could walk, but only with a limp. And it was painful — something was wrong with his stretched leg, and his back hurt from the "hanging." He turned to Batu and Nyam and faced reality.

"I cannot go on as before. I doubt if I can ride a horse."

Batu responded as if he had been waiting for this confession, "Yes, that is true, but we can't leave you here. Nyam and I have been working on a plan." and he pulled out a map, taken from Smiley's car. Nyam joined them under the shelter, and Batu outlined the plan.

"The map shows that we are near the village of Bogdo, which about ninety kilometers from Bayanhongor, on the main road to Altai and then to the prison just outside Tolbo." Batu leaned back, relaxed, and looked at Uno. "Transportation can be arranged on the main road, and you have the proper papers." Batu smiled, "And as for your share of the money, you can tell Major Bagana that we are arriving in Bulgan as you speak — that we have been delivered — because the timing should be about right. By the time you arrive back at URBAD, we should be approaching Bulgan."

Nyam suggested, "You might want to explain your condition and the loss of Sergeant Dorvaa as an encounter with road bandits."

Batu added, "When you say this, watch the Major's face."

Uno accepted the plan with relief. He was tired and injured, and still had the feeling that he was expendable. Maybe returning to URBAD would be his salvation. He knew enough to force the Major to give him a share of the money, and he would be safe in the prison. His enlistment was about up, and he would return home to Hanh and sell shoes or something. As he thought this over, he listened to Batu and Nyam chatting by the campfire.

Batu looked into a small signaling mirror and asked, "Do you think this broken nose adds a little character to my face?"

"I don't know about character, Batu," Nyam responded. "I have noticed that your nose is bent to the left. I expect you'll be walking in circles, if you aren't careful."

And they both laughed. Uno smiled to himself, shook his head, and thought of Batu and Nyam's truly indomitable spirit, which drew people to them. It was no wonder that Willie's crew had survived in the treacherous environment of the URBAD prison. Just being with them a few days, he felt a part of their camaraderie.

THE NEXT MORNING, THEY redistributed the provisions and gently eased Uno into the saddle of the calmest mare. Batu would ride bareback.

"How does it feel?" Batu asked.

"Hurts all over," Uno responded in his scratchy voice, "But my foot is warm."

Batu had fashioned a "bootie" from a blanket to go over his foot, with the rope sandal on the outside. Uno appreciated the gesture.

They rode past a small highland lake on the trail to Bogdo, and stopped to water the horses and rest Uno's aching body. The lake was jumping with fish going after mayflies. A fishhawk glided overhead, and small brown thrushes worked their way through the brush along the bank. The smell of wood smoke was in the air, and it was warmer than it had been for a long time. Uno rested his bad leg against a log and looked out on the lake, feeling lucky to be alive.

He spoke to his companions in a tortured whisper, "I think they are going to betray you."

Batu and Nyam looked at him earnestly.

Uno continued, "There didn't seem to be a shred of sincerity in their conversations about your deal about buying enlistment into the army. They joked about it, said 'Let's enlist them in the Mongolian Navy as well,' and laughed. They are going to kill you and take the money."

Batu and Nyam were silent, thinking about what had been said.

Batu said, almost to himself, "I thought it was a good plan."

Nyam watched the jumping fish, shrugged and said, "Well, it's good to be warned. We knew we weren't dealing with the church choir."

Batu laughed and sadly shook his head.

They rode until evening, not making very good time, and decided on a cold camp, no fire, as they had seen lights on the hillside and could still smell wood smoke. As they neared Bogdo, the area was more populated. They made Uno a bed with the saddle blankets.

As they lay in their sleeping bags and saddle blankets, watching the stars overhead, Batu made a request. "Uno, we have a favor to ask."

Uno looked at him and waited, wondering what this was about.

"We want to know about Willie. We want to know how he is doing after this deal, and anything else you can tell us about the prison situation."

Uno considered the request. "How will I get a message to you?"

"Onor's mother, Udaa Sartaq, is well known in Dalanzadgad. You could send a message to her.

Uno considered Batu's request for only a moment before saying, "I'll be glad to do it. It's the least I can do."

THE NEXT MORNING, THEY rode into the village of Bogdo, which consisted of a dozen buildings and three yurts, with about twenty dogs and a few goats patrolling the single, muddy main street. There was a small park in town, with an open-air market and a trough for watering horses. They loosened the cinches on the saddles and let the horses drink as they looked around, worrying about Army patrols.

Nyam spoke. "I'll go to the market while you two water the horses. Both of you look a little scary."

Batu chuckled as he looked at Nyam through his blackened eyes and broken nose, and said, "Nyam, my friend Uno and I will recover. However, you will always look scary."

Uno, heartened by the thought that he might recover, suggested in his tortured whisper, "Maybe you could get us some fruit."

As he looked across the street, Batu gave a small start, and said, "Mother of God, I must be having a nightmare. I thought I saw Grandfather Khentii in that truck over there, but it may be another horse trader." He started walking slowly, in an unthreatening way, over to the old man in a truck with horses in the back.

Nyam waited to see that Batu was, in fact, walking in a straight line, then left for the market. Uno watched the horses to keep them from drinking too much, and thought of his future. Batu returned after a long conversation, in a very good mood.

It was arranged, and it was a stroke of luck. Khentii, the old horse trader, was going all the way to Altai, and was glad to have some company, especially if Uno would help with fuel costs. He would leave in a few hours. When Nyam returned from the market with bread, meat, canned fruit and carrots, they sorted gear and provisions on the grass, careful to conceal their weaponry. There were a few moments of silence as they looked at the bloodstained wallet that belonged to Dos. Then Uno looked around to assure privacy, and handed Batu a hand grenade.

"Here," Uno said, "You may need this. I found it in Smiley's car and carried in my coat."

Nyam responded with a start, "Shit, you carried this bomb with you? I lassoed you with a grenade in your pocket?"

Batu was also shocked. They were horsemen. They did not like grenades.

Uno, somewhat amused, said "It has double pins on the spoon. But you can pull the pins out quickly if need be."

Batu offered, "You can carry the bomb, Nyam."

Nyam responded, "Ah, no. Don't have room."

They compromised by putting the grenade on a packhorse. They ate canned sliced peaches from China and black bread, as they waited for the old trader to come by. The peaches tasted wonderful on Uno's injured throat.

As they ate, Batu peered at Uno with his glittering black eyes, and asked, "Uno, is there anything else that we should know? Something perhaps, that may save our lives?"

"I've been thinking about this," Uno responded. "There should be two Army officers who will be waiting for you at the building in Bulgan. Supposedly, the front doors of the building will be open, so you can see them, Supposedly, the money will be delivered to you by Willie's courier, who Willie says is the very best in the business. Willie said his man will be on the trail, to deliver the money as you near the building."

Uno scratched at his sore neck and continued, "You're supposed to take the money in and make the exchange, 25,000 U.S. dollars for bona fide enlistment papers in the Army. These officers have been part of the deal from the start, friends of Major Bagana, who handled the whole affair."

Then Uno seemed to relax, the whole story delivered, and said, "My role, along with Sergeant Dorvaa, was to make sure you did not bolt with the money. That amount of money can buy a lot in this country. You can be sure that you will be watched closely from the time you receive the money, maybe with long guns."

It was at this point that the old horse trader drove up, and they loaded Uno aboard and said their goodbyes.

Batu mentioned, "If you could tell Willie that we are okay, we would appreciate it very much. And please let us know how he is doing if you can."

Then Batu and Nyam said farewell and went to their horses.

As the truck pulled away and headed for Altai, Uno thought of Batu's words, "Tell Willie that we are okay," and it made him sad. He was convinced that Batu and Nyam would be dead in a few days.

Uno thought about why he was drawn to them so. He felt they had a combination of rare characteristics. Foremost, they were humble, and though talented in many ways, they didn't let their egos cause them to overreach and make bold assumptions. Secondly, they had empathy for those around them, and consequently saw and understood more of the daily events of life. And third, what made it all work, they were brutally honest in their assessment of themselves and others. They did not delude themselves one iota. Uno truly felt that it had been a privilege to know them in what was to be their short lives. They had been good to him.

Chapter 11
Across the Gobi

As the old trader's truck pulled out for Altai with Uno aboard, Batu and Nyam left Bogdo, making good time on the road that ran southeast for about thirty kilometers before turning back southwest, leaving them back on an overland trail. They were watching their back.

Batu glanced back and said, "See anything, Nyam?"

Nyam responded, "No, we have been very lucky. No flying roadblocks yet, and hardly anyone along the road. Of course, we are headed for the Gobi Desert."

Riding steadily, they left the trail at dusk and found a good campsite in a small ravine on a side hill, protected from the wind.

They sat by a small campfire and ate black bread and small green grapes that Nyam had purchased in the market. The grapes were moist and delicious, and were very rarely found in Mongolia. Batu and Nyam relished the new foods.

As they relaxed, Batu appraised the horses. "Aren't these good horses, Nyam? The gray that I'm riding follows me around like a puppy."

Nyam laughed. "Of course she does, you've been feeding her carrots."

"Yes, but I've been feeding them all carrots."

Seriously, Batu asked, "Do you think we'll do okay in the Mongolian Army?

Nyam responded, "I don't know about the army, Batu. As I have said, I'm very tired of killing people. I just want to be with Onor."

Batu thought about this. "Well, we will just make it happen, if we can."

THE NEXT DAY WAS SPENT climbing a high ridge and they had to change out horses often. The extra water they were carrying was a heavy burden on the animals. They finally broke over the crest of the ridge and Nyam spoke. "Whoa. What is that?"

Batu stared in disbelief. "It looks like a huge wall coming toward us."

Nyam started pulling the horse leads closer. "We better find shelter. I think it's a monster sandstorm."

Batu looked, then he looked again, and said, "Yes. Lightning in the distance, rain, and wind. Maybe we can find shelter on the side hill to protect the horses."

There was nothing behind them, so they rode quickly down the ridge, looking for an L-shaped ravine that would offer some protection from the wind. They saw a ravine and started towards it when they found an old tree near the ravine that could be used to secure the horses and provide them with some overhead protection from a possible hailstorm. As the wind started howling, they discussed their location.

"Do you think inside the ravine would be better?" Batu asked, "It would be better protection from this wind."

Nyam agreed.

Just then the fury of the storm hit and the horses started spooking.

"Too late," Batu said. "We are stuck here, I'll get the horses secured, at least we can tie them easier here."

The rain came, with lightning and blowing sand.

Batu yelled, "I didn't know sand could blow in a rainstorm."

Lightning and tremendous thunderclaps exploded around them, with the sound bouncing off the hills to hit them in shock waves. The horses were terrified by the explosions but were firmly held in check by the horsemen.

"We should have camped in the ravine," Batu hollered over the noise.

Nyam nodded as he patted a nervous horse. The rain came in torrents, and they didn't have a chance to make a shelter. They huddled by the old tree and waited. Just before dusk, there was a roaring sound in addition to all the other noises, and they looked at each other in wonder. Then as the ground shook, a raging wall of water came roaring down the ravine beside them. They stared in disbelief.

"It's a flash flood!" Batu hollered over the noise, as they watched the turbulent stream wash out everything before it.

Nyam yelled, "Good thing we never made it to the ravine."

"Like Willie says," Batu responded, "The Lord protects fools."

The next morning, the ravine looked dry and unthreatening, but Batu and Nyam peered at if as if it were full of snakes.

"Who would have thought of that little ditch as a death trap," Batu said. Nyam just shook his head.

AS THEY RODE SOUTHEAST, the country started changing, with less vegetation and lower hills. It was much warmer. They were entering the heart of the Great Gobi Desert. The weather was clear and calm after the storm and small delicate flowers were sprouting, as desert plants do after a rain. Off to the right, an escarpment rose out of the desert floor, and in the distance, large birds soared back and forth in the thermals.

They traded out horses often, to keep them from overtiring, and maintained a steady pace in the heat. Not used to the warmth, they grew sleepy, so to stay awake, they started reminiscing about playing polo in China.

"Being in the Chinese army was bad, but I liked our life as polo players. We played well, and we were treated well," Nyam commented, thinking of the good times they had at General Tang's villa, which had often resembled a bus station, with card games, polo team meetings, and bull sessions going on at all hours. General Tang was a benevolent host for "his boys" and often directed Sergeant Geo Chee, his driver and world-class dog robber, to get them anything they wanted. Chee was renown for his ability to procure or "fix" almost anything. He was a much-treasured asset.

"Do you remember," Nyam said, "the night you broke up the poker game?"

Batu responded immediately, "Yes, Nyam, I remember," grimacing and rolling his eyes.

"Well, if you don't mind, Batu, I would like to hear the story again," laughed Nyam, and he began, as if he were telling a crowd of listeners. "There we were, playing a late-night card game with General Tang, Sergeant Chee, myself, of course, and the General's woman, the wonderful Illia."

Batu said again, "Nyam, I've heard this story many times. And I was there."

As they rode down the grade, past the escarpment, Nyam continued his story as if he had not heard Batu's comment. "You will recall, Batu," he smiled, "that you were sitting that game out, improving your English by reading a copy of Illia's Cosmopolitan magazine that had been bootlegged from the American Embassy."

Nyam continued, as this was his favorite part. "Remember? Tang had poured glasses of baijiu all around. Chee was leaning back in his chair, dealing the cards over his big belly. Illia was enjoying a cheroot as she checked her hand."

"Just as Tang took a healthy drink of baijiu, you asked Illia if it was true that oral sex improved a relationship!" Nyam laughed at the memory. "Chee dumped the cards as his chair fell over backwards. Tang spit his drink all over the table and Illia laughed so hard she dropped her cheroot on her new tablecloth." Then Nyam added, as he laughed, "Me, I was embarrassed."

Batu responded as he laughed, despite himself, "You were not embarrassed, Nyam, you enjoyed every moment of that evening. You know, I really didn't understand what I was saying. Did you?"

Nyam laughed again and said, "Those were indeed good times."

Suddenly serious, Batu asked, "Those were our friends. Have you ever wondered why they made no effort to get us out of that hellhole? URBAD is not really a recognized prison, it's a dumping ground where no one returns. Why did they leave us there?"

Nyam could tell that Batu was really disturbed by the idea that they had been abandoned in the unknown backside of Mongolia. It was not in keeping with his sense of propriety.

They rode quietly as the terrain became flatter and they moved from the escarpment into high desert, with less vegetation, and heat building up off the sand. They nurtured the horses as best they could, changing mounts often. On the third day of riding from Bogdo, they came across a dry stream bed, and dug down in the sand for water. At about 1 meter, the sand grew damp, so they kept digging as far as they could reach, but they didn't find water. That night they made a very dry camp beside the hole in the ground, out of the wind, and went to sleep uneasily, thinking about flash floods.

TWO DAYS LATER, IN the afternoon, they approached their destination, Bulgan, from the west. Since the only road into the village was from the other side, they circled the village, cautiously checking it out. Once again, there was a building on the outskirts of the village, much like the setup in Sharga that had cost Dos his life. Parked in the back of the building was a small, camouflaged truck with a canvas cover over the back. No one was in sight.

Batu shook his head in disbelief as they looked at the scene, and said, "This looks like the ambush site in Sharga. Can you believe this?"

Nyam nodded, "We had better be very careful."

They decided to stop and camp out one more night, to observe the building and make a plan. As they huddled in the cold camp near a depression in the desert, they discussed options.

"We need to approach the village from the road side to give Willie's runner a chance to give us the money. No doubt, he is set up just off the approach road." Batu said.

Nyam agreed, "There are banks on both sides of the road and juniper trees, so he could be anywhere. We have to go down the road. How do you think he will hand off the money?"

"No idea," Batu answered, "But Willie said he is very creative, and we may never see him."

So the next morning, Batu and Nyam, with their hearts in their mouths, rode slowly down the road toward Bulgan, approaching the outbuilding in the distance. They wore no hats, so they would be recognizable to Willie's runner. As they walked their horses along the road, the horses started pulling right, toward a bucket nearly concealed by a bush. Batu and Nyam reined in their mounts, trying to keep them on the road, but the thirsty horses smelled water in the bucket and pushed ahead. The bucket, to their amazement, had "Batu" written on its side.

As they stared unbelievably at the bucket, they noticed a wire stretched tightly from the bucket up the bank to their right. The thirsty horses continued to drink the water. Then they heard a singing sound as a heavy satchel came sliding down the wire and crashed into the bucket of water, causing the horses to rear up in panic. The money had been delivered.

Picking up the satchel, Batu muttered, "The runner is a genius. He knew the thirsty horses would be drawn to the water — and who would have thought of a wire to deliver the satchel? He is long gone, and I would say, he earned his pay from Willie."

They opened the satchel and tore loose a brown wrapper that revealed many, many American dollars. Batu looked at Nyam.

"Tempting to take the money and run, but we wouldn't get far on tired horses, and I'm sure the URBAD crew are watching us."

As if on cue, they heard a shrill whistle, a signal used in army maneuvers. They looked toward the sound and saw the Mongolian flag flying high from a lanyard at the outbuilding. The front doors were open. Just inside, two army officers in dress uniform were sitting at a table, facing out.

The message was clear: Come on in and join the army, and give us the $25,000 cash.

Batu and Nyam took all of this in. They looked thoughtfully at each other.

"Maybe this deal is legitimate, after all," Batu said.

Nyam, wanting to believe, said, "They certainly seem well organized. Look at those uniforms. They look very official."

The building was still pretty far away, so they moved forward to get a better look. They figured binoculars had been on them, prompting the signal from such a distance. URBAD knew they had the money.

"So," Batu asked his partner, "You want to keep going and feel them out?"

"Yes, but with caution," Nyam answered. "Let's ride with the satchel between us, so they know if they shoot one of us, the other runs with the money."

Batu nodded. "Gruesome, but good thinking."

They rode toward the building, ready to bolt, but saw nothing.

Batu noted, "The truck is around the corner from the front door, but still located so we can see part of it. Why did they park it that way? To assure us?"

"Yes, I'm worried about the truck, too," Nyam answered.

They walked their horses toward the front of the building, knowing they would have to dismount soon. Their weapons were at the ready. As they rode closer, they watched the army officers, who continued to sit at the table looking out at them. Batu and Nyam cautiously dismounted, dropped the reins, and walked to the front of the building.

Nyam commented, "They certainly are relaxed."

As they got closer, Batu said with a small catch in his voice, "They aren't relaxed, Nyam, they're dead! I just saw a fly come out of one guy's mouth!"

Then they heard the tailgate of the truck drop, and the snicking sound of a bolt, being slid home.

Batu yelled as he pushed Nyam into the building, "Get down, get down, get down! They are going to air out the building!"

As they scrambled, looking for cover, the gun started chattering. Bullets started stitching through the side of the building, all around them.

Batu yelled again, "This is how cowards kill people — they machine gun their building!"

The rounds were popping around them and there was little cover, so they pushed the dead army officers onto the floor and got down behind the bodies. Nyam was too big to hide behind a body, and Batu heard him get hit and grunt, then heard him get hit again. The rounds kept coming, shooting the building to pieces, even blowing apart the satchel of money. The shooting went on and on, and the building was coming apart.

The gunners stopped to change belts, and Batu asked, "Nyam, you hit bad?"

"Twice, but don't know, "Nyam answered, and the firing started again.

After what seemed forever, the gunners stopped, to change belts again. The firing had been so intense that Batu and Nyam didn't stand a chance. They couldn't move without being hit. But finally, it stopped, and they lay still, waiting, making no sounds.

Batu whispered, "Be ready. They are so fucking greedy, they'll come for the money soon."

They laid very still, waiting, and finally heard laughter from outside the building. They saw two shadows as Major Bagana and the Russian from Dansk that had been Willie's new bodyguard, walked smugly across the threshold, looking at the shot-up satchel in the middle of the floor.

Nyam was ready, and opened up with the machine pistol, stitching the Major across the chest, causing him to do a little death dance right there in the doorway. Batu was now worried about Nyam, because his technique with the machine pistol was sloppy, not like Nyam at all. The Major went down and the Russian lurched back out the doorway, but Nyam corrected and shot a short little burst that blew the back of the Russian's head off.

The machine gunners in the truck started firing frantically again when they saw the Russian go down. Nyam watched, astonished, as Batu timed the sweep of the gun, stood up and walked out the front door, just barely around the corner from the gunners, and called his horse.

His gray, the horse that followed him like a puppy, came running during the lull, and Batu pulled the grenade off the saddle and smacked the gray to get her out of harm's way. But as the horse moved away from the house, the movement attracted the nervous gunners and they swung the gun on the horse, killing her.

Batu, enraged, ran along the edge of the house, and as the gun swung toward him, one gunner yelled, "Grenade!" just before the explosion killed them. Batu stepped over the dead Russian to get to his horse that lay dying, and hung his head.

As Nyam lay on the floor, bleeding from his wounds, Batu came through the door to check on him. While walking toward him through the wreckage, Batu kicked the satchel viciously, scattering $100 bills across the room.

"Those motherfuckers killed my horse."

Chapter 12
Batu Driving?

Batu knew they needed to keep moving because of all the gunfire and carnage, bodies lying all over the place. He moved quickly to Nyam, who had propped himself against the remnants of the table. The corpses of the two army officers were staring at them like ghouls, their bodies pierced by many machine gun rounds.

As Batu examined Nyam's wounds, still angry about his horse, he snapped, "Couldn't you have laid flatter?"

Nyam winced and answered, "I am not a midget like you, Batu."

Batu started a commentary about Nyam's wounds, "High on the shoulder, it plowed a trough along the back of your shoulder." He looked down and continued, "The leg wound looks like a ricochet, like a deep scrape. But both are bleeding too much."

He sat back on his haunches, amid the rubble, bodies and blood — with his blackened eyes, broken nose and ragged clothes, he looked like a refugee from an A-bomb blast.

"We must get you to a doctor in Dalanzadgad. I will drive you there in the truck."

Nyam stared at Batu and said, "You're going to drive?"

Batu nodded and moved through the wreckage toward the door.

Raising his voice, Nyam asked again, "You're going to drive?"

Batu didn't respond, as he left to bring the truck around to the front door. As Nyam waited, he thought of Batu's driving. Batu was a terrible driver. He was worse than terrible. He was dangerous. Nyam reasoned that he might be better off laying here, bleeding out, than riding with Batu.

Then he heard the over-revving of the engine and the grinding of gears, and said to himself, "Oh shit. Here we go."

Meanwhile, Batu was carefully angling across to the front door, grinding the gears of the piece-of-shit army truck, trying to shift. He hit the corner of the small porch, causing the bullet-riddled support column to collapse on the truck, putting a large dent in the hood and stalling the engine. Batu, unfazed, scooted through the wreckage and helped Nyam cross the littered floor to the passenger side of the truck. Then he gathered up the money and dumped the shot-up satchel unceremoniously on the floorboard in front of Nyam. Moving quickly, he stripped the saddle and gear off of his dead horse. Nyam's horse was gone. Batu checked on Nyam.

"You okay?"

Nyam responded with a grimace. He was bleeding. Batu handed him pieces of blanket to use as bandages. He started the truck, and rather than trying to find reverse, just bounced through the porch wreckage and out to the road to where the pack horses were tied. Batu quickly stripped the packs off and tied the horses on long leads to the back of the truck.

"We can't go fast or far with the horses like this, but we'll have them if this damn machine quits," he explained.

And they were off, with the horses trotting behind. Batu managed to stay on the road for a while without incident, putting some distance between them and Bulgan. They were lucky, the area was remote, and no one was around. Batu was very concerned about Willie and Cheech after the Russian's treachery and couldn't concentrate on driving.

Batu said, "We must stop and tend to your wounds, then decide what to do."

"What to do?" Nyam asked.

"Yes," Batu said, "If we can't stop the bleeding, we'll have to go all the way in to Dalandzadgad tonight, and this piece-of-shit army truck has only one light."

Batu continued for another few kilometers, looking keenly, then abruptly turned off the road, up over the crest of a small hill, a good place to hide.

Batu made a pallet in the bloodstained bed of the truck. He had unceremoniously dumped the bodies of the horse-killing machine gunners in the yard, and the machine gun on top of them, with absolutely no remorse.

Batu made a new bandage for Nyam's shoulder, fashioned a tourniquet for the leg wound, cautioning him to loosen it occasionally, gave him some water, and left. Nyam tended the tourniquet and lay quietly, wondering what happened to Batu. Then Batu appeared before him, carrying a large ball of spider webs.

"Whoa," Nyam exclaimed.

Batu smiled. "We will stuff these spider webs into your wounds, it should stop the bleeding."

Nyam curled up his lip, like old times, and asked, "Is that very sanitary?"

Batu laughed, "What are you worried about? You're probably going to bleed to death, anyway."

"To tell you the truth, I thought your driving would have killed us by now." Nyam responded.

Batu countered, very glad that Nyam felt well enough to banter, "You're a big, ugly, comedian, Nyam, and you can be assured that if you die, I won't piss on your grave, because I never want to stand in line again."

The spider web pack seemed to stop the bleeding and the tourniquet was loosened a bit, so they decided to rest for a while as the sun was setting. The adrenalin had worn off, they were exhausted, and both fell into a restless sleep as they listened to the horses moving around in the brush.

BATU WOKE WITH A START, rolled over and loosened the tourniquet. He examined Nyam's wounds by match light. They felt moist, so he lit a candle to look closer. Nyam was bleeding again and lay very still.

He shook Nyam awake, and asked, "Are you cold?"

"Yes," Nyam answered quietly, and curled up into a ball on the blankets.

Batu was worried that Nyam was bleeding to death, and he could do nothing about it. It was too dark to drive, with only one weak light on the treacherous road. Batu was frustrated and near panic. What could he do to save his friend? He walked over the small hill, thinking. Maybe a compression bandage would work. Then he stopped, looked at the road, then at the horizon, and a smile began that hurt his broken nose. He turned and shuffled back to the truck.

"Nyam, did I ever tell you how lucky we are?"

Nyam groaned groggily, "I don't feel that we are so lucky, right now."

Batu smiled, in spite of the pain. "We are lucky my friend. What we have out there is a 'bombers moon.' You can read a newspaper in the moonlight. We are driving to Dalanzadgad now. To the hospital." Batu went on, excited at their deliverance, "Let's get you into the front seat, because the ride may be a little rough."

As they gingerly moved Nyam from the bed of the truck, Nyam confessed, "I'm scared."

Batu froze. He couldn't conceive of Nyam being afraid of anything.

"You are afraid of dying?"

Nyam gave a coughing laugh, "No, you idiot, I'm afraid of your driving."

Batu called out over his shoulder as he went to cut the horses loose, "Well, maybe you'll bleed to death on the way, and I won't have to listen to your complaints about my driving."

And so the journey to Dalanzadgad began. It was indeed a wild ride. Nyam, wedged in the front seat and bleeding, coached Batu on the fine art of double clutching as he shifted the gears of the beastly truck. Although the horses were free, they followed along behind the bouncing truck for a while before being outdistanced. Maybe it was the carrots.

The huge full moon hung in the sky above them like a monster streetlamp, lighting up the roadway almost clear as day. It was quiet in the high desert, except for the rattling of the diesel engine. Batu, for all his superb horsemanship, couldn't master the art of driving. He literally steered from ditch to ditch, all night long. He seemed incapable of anticipating the movement of the vehicle and was always late to respond. Nyam watched him, amazed, and fearing he might have a nervous breakdown before he bled to death, shut his eyes tight and held on. Fortunately, there was no traffic on the lonely road.

They finally entered the city, glowing ghostly in the moonlight just before dawn, and had no trouble finding the hospital. It was a large block structure with an immaculate lawn and a well-marked emergency entrance. There was no one about. Batu managed to park the truck without hitting anything, then laid his hand on Nyam's shoulder to wake him. No response.

Batu hastily felt Nyam's weak pulse as he spoke to him, "Nyam, wake up! We are at the hospital." Still no response or movement.

Very concerned, Batu bailed out of the truck and tried the emergency entrance door. It was locked, and there was no response to his pounding. Batu pulled out his pistol and fired five evenly timed shots into the air, the universal signal for distress or danger.

Moments later, a sleepy looking orderly peered cautiously at the apparition standing in the driveway, motioning him to help with a wounded man. The world over, emergency room types have seen just about everything, and he responded quickly, coming with a gurney to move Nyam inside.

The on-duty physician and nurses worked on Nyam quickly to stop the bleeding, then sent the orderly back out to find out more about the accident. The orderly returned shortly with a glove stuffed with $1000 of tattered bills and a note. It read, "Thank you very much. Please take this money for the care and feeding of your new guest." The orderly had found it on the reception desk, and no one was there.

BATU WANTED TO DUMP the truck. He wanted no questions from the hospital or the police, surely to be drawn by the gunfire. The satchel of money would raise more questions. He wanted to find a field of high grass, drive into it, and comb the grass back up to hide the truck. But it was still too dark to find a field, so he drove the back streets with his one light shining. His driving was getting better; he hadn't hit anything lately.

Just as dawn was breaking, he saw an abandoned building. It looked like a brick plant, with crumbling walls and falling roof beams laying askew. He managed to wedge the truck into the back corner by an old kiln with a chimney full of bats, just returning from their nightly forays. Batu smiled as he thought of the perfect place to hide the money. He crawled into the kiln, and could smell the stench and feel the heat from the fermenting bat guano in the bottom of the chimney. The smell was awful. Roaches were scurrying everywhere, and the bats were screaming at the intruder. Batu gagged as he scooped out a hole to bury the satchel in the stinking, roach-infested bat shit. He thought, *I may not come back for this money.*

He now traveled light and moved quickly, keeping only one pistol and a dagger. He sadly had to leave the coveted, but now blood-soaked sleeping bags. He looked and smelled awful, and could still feel roaches crawling over him. As he wandered the side streets, he came upon a small park where an old man was filling water buckets from a manual water pump with a long handle. Batu stood at a respectful distance, waiting for the old man to fill the buckets.

The man sniffed, noticed him and said, "Whoa. My god, man, stand still!" and he threw both buckets of water over Batu, who stood there, smiling. Then the old man asked, "What did you step in, boy?"

Batu laughed. "You wouldn't believe it if I told you. Thank you for the bath, Grandfather." Then Batu asked, "By chance, could I buy you some breakfast?"

The old man, whose name was Rekap, said "My friend, I think you do not know how bad you look. Even my restaurant — where I am well known, I might add — would not allow us to sit at their tables."

He laughed as he said this, with a twinkle in his eyes. Then he said, "It looks like you've had a hard time lately, but I sense you are a good soul. Regarding your generous offer of a breakfast, I propose that instead of rushing in dirty for a snack, we get you cleaned up and into some decent clothes — and stroll into the restaurant for a decent meal. What do you say?"

By this time, Batu was laughing as well, and said, "I can see you are a man of good taste and wisdom, and I'm looking forward to learning about what's going on in Dalanzadgad."

SO BATU AND REKAP HAD an excellent breakfast at a local restaurant, and Batu learned where good lodging could be found nearby. He also learned that Udaa Sartaq, Onor's mother, was well known as a translator in the city. She knew five or six languages, Rekap told him, and she was so proficient that she translated legal contracts. She was much in demand in this multicultural city, as well as other countries.

Batu had known her in the old days, when she was a translator for General Tang. He remembered that she was a good mother, widowed, and took Onor everywhere with her. He remembered that Geo Chee, Tang's dog robber and fixer, was sweet on her, and always nearby.

Batu developed a plan. He would get lodging, rest, and lay low for a while, so Nyam could recover. He would wait and observe, to see if anyone from URBAD was still in pursuit. Then, if there were no guards on Nyam, he would pick him up and they would go see Onor and her mother. By that time, maybe Uno would have sent a message about Willie's condition, and the situation at the prison. And they would take it from there.

The city of Dalanzadgad had no less than six roads entering it from all directions. Batu sat in his rented room overlooking the village square, and, for hours, watched the people going back and forth conducting their business of the day. He tried to imagine what their lives were like. He was wistfully envious, and hoped he could have a life like any one of them, someday.

Chapter 13
Reunion

After three days, Batu decided to check on Nyam. He figured Nyam, with his strong constitution, might be up and around already. He carefully approached the hospital, looking for army types or police guards, and saw none. Ever cautious, he entered a side door and roamed the halls, looking for anything unusual, until he was stopped by a nurse who had been on duty the night they arrived, who told him Nyam was in the courtyard below, getting some sunshine.

Much relieved that Nyam was doing okay, Batu sped down the spiral staircase and approached the courtyard. He rounded the corner and saw the huge figure of Nyam hunched over a table. But Mother of God, he looked terrible! His face was emaciated, and he was swathed in bandages. Batu was shocked and his mouth went dry. His friend was obviously at death's door. Batu grabbed his stomach and slowly turned away. He was not ready for this.

Then he heard Nyam's "card-playing chuckle" and looked again at his friend, and saw that it was not Nyam at all — rather, a similar-sized, older, beat-up version of Nyam, who was semi-reclining on the other side, playing poker with the old man. Batu was so relieved that he just stood there breathing deep, until Nyam noticed him and spoke the words that Batu had heard many times.

"Batu! You okay?"

Batu felt his eyes misting as he answered, "Yeah, Nyam, I'm alright, but you don't look so good."

Nyam answered, "Well, I've got a good hand, I might actually win this one. Meet Grandfather Chug. He was in a car wreck. You should think about that, the way you drive."

Nyam had lost a lot of blood, but luckily had little infection, in spite of the spider web packs. He had been given more than three liters of blood and was weak but recovering. They estimated discharge in another three days. No police or army types had come around. Apparently, this was a very lively city and their arrival had been unnoticed. Also, it looked like the thousand dollars cash had bought them some anonymity, not an unusual thing in this part of the world. They were lucky.

Their plan was simple. Batu and Nyam would wait until they were ready, then they would simply take a taxi to Udaa Sartaq's villa in the outskirts of the city. They would arrive unannounced, to enable them to evaluate the situation, and either stop or keep on going. They learned that Udaa had been very successful. In fact, she was quite an entrepreneur, running greenhouses of potted plants and mulched soil, and even a small trucking line.

Eight days after entering the hospital, Nyam was discharged, although still very weak. As the orderly pushed his wheelchair toward the front door, Batu, as was his habit, cautiously rerouted their exit out the service entrance to a waiting taxi, and over to Batu's room.

Finally, after another three days of resting, sleeping and eating, they felt they were ready to see Udaa and Onor. Nyam was nervous.

"Suppose she's already married, or she doesn't love me?"

Batu couldn't resist. "Well, I can certainly understand either one of those situations," he smiled, "But I think you'll be fine."

Batu and Nyam looked pretty good. They had new clothes, and they were cleaner than they'd ever been in their life — enjoying the indoor shower immensely.

THE TAXI THEY TOOK to Udaa's villa was an old Mercedes Benz with an engine that rattled like the old truck, but they liked its darkened windows. They only had one gun between them, and no grenades, thank God, but they still felt pretty good. Maybe it was because they were so clean. They didn't expect trouble.

Udaa's villa was beautiful, perched on the side of the hill, with a great view of the valley and exquisite landscaping. It was made of stone and glass, with traditional Mongolian architecture blended in artistically. No one was around, but toward the back of the villa, what looked like a Chinese government staff car was parked. Nyam was visibly nervous.

Batu commented, "I haven't seen you this nervous, even in gunfights." He added, enjoying himself, "Just remember, no cussing, or farting, or picking your nose. Mind your manners."

Nyam just looked at him and shook his head.

Batu advised the taxi driver, "Park at an angle, so we can leave quickly if we have to."

The driver's eyes grew large. What was he getting into? They waited to be recognized, with the engine still running. After a moment, Udaa appeared at the door, looked at the darkened taxi, and took a few steps forward. No Onor.

Nyam muttered, "Shit, Onor's probably married and has five kids."

Batu rolled down the passenger windows slowly, so Udaa could see him, and spoke. "Udaa, it's me, Batu, and Nyam," and waited for a response.

Udaa took three steps toward the taxi, peered at them unbelievingly, and fainted, pitching forward into the rose garden. Batu and Nyam ran to Udaa's aid, kneeling and trying to revive her, and to fish her out of the roses without cutting her up. Then the front door opened, and a figure stood over them, staring with his mouth open. It was Geo Chee, Udaa's long-time boyfriend.

Batu's response to this new arrival was astonishing. He swung from the ground up in a roundhouse arc, and as he rose, delivered a mighty punch to Chee, knocking him flat on his back near the front steps. Witnessing all of this, the taxi driver peeled out of the driveway in his Mercedes and knocked down the mailbox as he left without getting paid.

Nyam looked at Batu, shook his head, and said, "Two down. Mind your manners, you said." He added, admiringly, "That was quite a punch."

Batu didn't hear him. He was standing over Chee, screaming at him, very angry.

"We are your friends, why did you leave us in that stinking hellhole?!" Then he leaned closer, and yelled again, "Why didn't you get us out of there?"

Geo Chee rubbed his jaw. "Batu! It's you! We thought both of you were dead." Then he sat up and added, "Ow. That was quite a punch."

Chapter 14
Bad News

A short time later, they stood in Udaa's large kitchen as she brewed a pot of tea. They looked at each other, taking stock, still not believing this turn of events. Udaa had cleaned up, with minor scratches, and Chee's jaw appeared to be working. Batu still wore a look of righteous indignation as he looked at Chee. Nyam leaned over the counter, watching the tea pot, and glanced around, looking. No Onor.

Udaa, a born negotiator, set out some pastries on the kitchen table, and started pouring tea all around. She wanted to settle them down. She knew Batu and Nyam were due an explanation, so she nodded to Chee and offered a suggestion.

"Why don't you tell them how we were deceived?"

Chee sighed and shook his head. He explained, "Since seeing you again, I am just now putting it together. I believe you made a terrible enemy in Major Khoo when you knocked him off that gun." Chee rubbed his jaw and continued, "He has many powerful friends, and his goal was to put an end to you, forever. An all-points dispatch went out to all army units that an URBAD prison vehicle had gone off a bridge on your way to prison, all hands lost, with you and Nyam aboard. Including Nyam must have been very satisfying for Khoo. He knew Nyam was your friend. He even had your records and a few personal effects returned to your unit. It was a nice touch. That Khoo is a conniving bastard. You called attention to his incompetence, and his career has stalled, even with all his connections."

Leaning towards them, Chee added very earnestly, "General Tang thought the world of you two. When he hears our news, he will be enraged at what has happened. Tang has gone far in the Chinese Army, just receiving his third star. I can say with assurance that we will do whatever we can to help you both."

Taking a bite of roll and a sip of tea, Chee shifted his chair, looked at Batu and asked, "Would you please tell me all that has happened, from the beginning? So I can write it down in detail, if that's okay?"

Batu relaxed, took a deep breath, and slowly told the story from the beginning.

WHILE BATU WAS RECOUNTING history, Nyam was more interested in the present, and as he looked around, Udaa caught his eye and said quietly, "Would you like to see Onor?"

Nyam stiffened and nodded, "Yes, I would."

They excused themselves, passed through the house to the back and got into a small garden truck parked at the back door. Udaa drove expertly, and stated, "We have some greenhouses up on a hill, for better sunshine in all directions. We had to winch the house parts up there for assembly. It was quite a project, and it's finally paying off. We pumped water up there and with all that sunlight..."

As Udaa talked, Nyam was thinking of Onor. Was it going to be this easy? Was he going to be able to take up where he had left off years ago? He was beginning to feel that it was a wonderful world. Maybe he had a future after all.

Then he heard Udaa's next sentence, "....she's up there at the greenhouses now with Sam, the new love of her life."

Nyam's stomach grabbed, and his "wonderful world" collapsed. She had a love of her life. She had Sam. Nyam was sick at heart, and wanted to jump from the truck. He looked at his feet and his mouth was dry. He did not know what to do.

Udaa drove up to the base of the hill, parked and killed the engine. There was a trail leading up to the greenhouses on the crest of the hill.

Nyam looked over at Udaa and muttered, "Maybe I should go."

Udaa didn't hear him. She was looking up at the greenhouses.

"There's Onor now. She must have seen the truck. She's with her new horse, Samantha."

Then Udaa looked over at the stunned Nyam, and added, "You know, she's absolutely crazy about you, and she never gave up hope. Not for one minute. I hope you are always good to her."

Nyam, almost numb at this point from the kaleidoscope of emotions; up, down, up again, slid out of the truck and leaned against the fender, looking up at Onor. He could tell when she recognized him. She jerked, almost as if she'd been shot. Then she abandoned the horse and started running down the hill at full speed. She was now a grown woman, and beautiful, with her open face and black hair streaming in all directions. She ran like he remembered, forward on the balls of her feet, with her hands swinging like paddles at her sides. He stood by the truck, finding it a little hard to breathe, watching as she ran out of her shoes, but kept coming like a small freight train.

She called out "Nyam Bear!" as she collided with him full force. Knocking him on his back with her on top, hugging him.

Both were lying in the dirt, laughing, and Nyam said between laughs, "You ran right out of your shoes!"

LATER THAT EVENING, Udaa and Batu were relaxing after dinner in the living room of the spacious villa, discussing recent events. Batu liked Udaa. He found her to be a kindred spirit, facing life with the same crystal-clear, hard-core realism as he did. She was a beautiful woman, with large, intelligent, almond-shaped eyes, and dark straight hair with a touch of gray. He guessed her age at forty-five, but had already learned you never ask a lady her age. She dressed well, in traditional Mongolian fashion, with a stylish flair. She had lost her husband in a border war years ago, and had concentrated on her expanding businesses and raising Onor. Her language skills as a translator were well known throughout Asia, allowing her easy passage across most borders. She was relaxed, good humored, and laughed a lot. Batu guessed she was wealthy, but she didn't act it. She had been Geo Chee's lover for many years.

In fact, Chee had told her of the event that had resulted in Batu's imprisonment, many years ago. Batu had been a loader on a huge 155-millimeter self-propelled gun, a maneuverable monster mounted on a track. Though he had a natural talent for operating it, Batu felt the gun was too loud, stank and tore up the earth. The gun crew had done well in drill evaluations and was scheduled to compete in a competitive firing exercise in front of the command bunker of the entire general staff. As the gun rolled into position to fire early that morning, an ambitious Major took over the gun to "make points" in front of the Generals in the bunker. The Major pointed, yelled and gestured, acting clearly in command as the gun rolled into position to fire at the target, one-quarter mile away.

And thus, the spectacle began. The Major, a self-appointed gun commander, pressed the fire button and the gun discharged — with the muzzle cover still on the barrel. The gun exploded, and Batu, the first loader, suffered only minor cuts, but the second loader was beheaded by the blow-back debris from the gun. His head rolled away from the gun, left a red path in the snow as straight as a croquet ball up through the view port of the command bunker, where it landed on the white table serving tea and goat-milk biscuits to the Generals. As the head quit rolling on the table with a surprised look on its face, the story was that one General soiled his pants, another vomited, and a promising young Lieutenant Colonel Aide passed out and was never seen again.

Batu, still on the gun and in a rage at the stupidity of the major, turned and knocked him off the track. The Major, whose name was Khoo, landed nine feet down on his face, breaking his jaw and causing lacerations on his face which required 127 stitches. Batu had struck an officer, and someone had to pay for this spectacle, so Batu was sent to the worst prison in Mongolia (with the help of the Major and his friends), and was not expected to survive.

Remembering this story, Udaa looked at the diminutive, innocent-looking Batu, and could hardly believe he was the source of such legends.

SERGEANT CHEE HAD DEPARTED earlier on his much-traveled trail to Chengdu, to report to General Tang with Batu's URBAD story in hand. As he left, he vowed again to "make things right" for Batu and Nyam. Udaa glanced at Nyam and Onor, out on the patio, talking earnestly to each other. She said to Batu, "I heard part of your story, and from the looks of Nyam's wounds and your face, you left a bloody trail on your way here."

Batu smiled at her. He really liked her coming-straight-at-you, no bullshit approach. He responded truthfully, "Yes, we left some messes behind us. I hope none of them rain down on you. Three dead in a ravine outside Sharga, and six dead in and around an old building outside Bulgan. Two of them were dead when we got there. I think all of this had to do with double crosses and treachery by the URBAD prison guard contingent, as there was $25,000 at stake. I stashed the money in a safe place for when we need it. I told Chee all of this. I think Nyam and I should leave the country."

"We don't know the URBAD prison situation," Batu continued, "whether they are still after us. We don't know the condition of Willie, our good friend whom you were told about. Hopefully we will get a message soon from Sargeant Erdene, a prison guard known to us as Uno, telling us what is happening. We helped him return to URBAD from Bogdo, after his fellow conspirators tried to kill him and we had some trouble with a swinging bridge."

Udaa smiled, shook her head and said, "Someday I would like to hear the whole story, start to finish."

She stood up, poured more tea, looked Batu in the eye and said, "I had a long conversation with Geo before he left. He is going to check your back trail and have it cleaned up, all the way to URBAD."

Batu asked, "He has that kind of reach, even in Mongolia?"

She nodded assuredly, "Oh yes, you would not believe the reach that General Tang and Chee have. And it's a lot more than just the army. You see, Tang's family goes back centuries as traders, and Tang is very much a part of that. We joke that the army is just a hobby for him. Borders mean nothing to the Tang dynasty. Trading everywhere is in their blood.

BATU WANTED TO BELIEVE in the reach of Tang and Chee to fix things, but still, as they waited, he set up on the trail to the villa every night with an AK-47 and a knife. Days passed, as they waited to hear from Chee or Uno. Nyam was quickly recovering from his wounds and was in high spirits. He and Onor were inseparable, spending long hours in the greenhouses.

One morning, Batu approached Udaa with a twinkle in his eye that she did not miss, "I know where there is a great source of fertilizer for your greenhouses. I saw it near town. Would you like to see?"

"Sure," she responded, "I'm always on the lookout for soil nutrients."

They piled into the truck and Udaa noticed shovels, gloves and head nets in the back. As she drove, she wondered, *"Head nets? What is Batu up to?"*

The old brickyard was still deserted, and Batu noticed that the truck had been stripped, and was barely recognizable. *"Good,"* he thought. They pulled up to the old brick kiln.

A few hours later, they were headed back to the villa in the small truck. The roach-and-bat-guano-infested satchel of money was on the floorboards at Batu's feet. Udaa, mortified at her own unladylike behavior, was spitting out the window every few minutes, and she shuddered as if she could feel the roaches crawling over her.

"Mother of God," she exclaimed, as she curled her upper lip up, causing Batu to smile, "The stench of that place was unbelievable." Then, after a moment of thinking about it, "That bat stuff is hot because it's <u>fermenting</u>?"

Batu had to laugh, admiring what a good sport Udaa had been, shoveling muck to help get to the satchel.

When they drove up to the courtyard in the back of the villa, Nyam was sitting on a deckchair with a stricken look on his face. Onor was nowhere around.

Udaa exited the truck, and with a gasp, asked "Onor?"

Nyam said, "No. She's raiding the basement for drinks. We got a message from Uno."

Batu approached him slowly. He knew it was bad news. "What?"

Nyam shook his head sadly. "Willie is dead. It seems that the Chinese called in their markers at all the prisons for drug smugglers, took them to Beijing, and executed them at halftime at a soccer match. Then they made the families of the smugglers pay for the bullets that killed them. Part of their war on drugs."

Batu folded his arms over his stomach and leaned forward, looking at the courtyard tiles. He was stunned. He thought the world of Willie, and had been worried about him because of their foiled escape, and all the money. He never thought about the goddamn Chinese. Shooting him at a soccer game — shit! And the fucking Chinese are supposed to be civilized!

The weather was surprisingly warm, and they sat in the courtyard and mourned the loss of Willie. They were depressed. Willie had been larger than life, and had taken care of them in that treacherous prison for years. It was his money in the satchel that precipitated their escape.

Onor returned from the basement with a wonderful drink that was new to them, scotch whiskey. It was so smooth that Batu thought he might enjoy becoming an alcoholic. Udaa and Onor were very sympathetic, and joined them in what was to become a wake. Nyam and Batu told many stories about Willie's smuggling, playing poker and improving life in the prison. Onor made numerous trips for more scotch, and she brought ice, which made it even better. Udaa brought them some comfort food, after taking what must have been her third shower.

Batu, feeling the scotch, asked Nyam, "Do you remember Willie's favorite toast? It seems sort of appropriate."

"Yes. He had many toasts. Was it the one about fast horses?"

"Yep." Batu nodded a little drunkenly. "It went like this. Willie would stand up and say: 'Here's to fast horses and pretty women.' And then he would say, 'The two things I love best are fast horses and pretty women. When I die, I want my hide tanned, and turned into a woman's saddle, so I can be between the two things I love best — fast horses and pretty women.'"

Then they drank another toast to Willie. And despite Batu's smell, Onor and Udaa put their hands on Batu's shoulders to comfort him.

THE NEXT MORNING, HUNG over, they discussed their future. Batu decided he didn't want to become an alcoholic after all. The general idea had been to get out of Asia and start their lives somewhere new. They had burned a lot of bridges and had made some powerful enemies. But now, Nyam had a compelling reason to stay in Mongolia; Onor, of course. But could he get away with it?

Batu asked Nyam the big question, "Nyam, do you want to stay here, if you can?"

Nyam answered with a smile, "Yes, I've been offered a position running a small trucking line. I think it's worth the risk of getting caught. If you want to stay, I'll let you load the trucks."

"Take the money as a wedding present and buy your freedom with it if you have to," Batu said. "My goal is to get out of here."

Udaa chimed in, "Money is not a problem, Batu. You keep that smelly, roach-infested money to fund your travels, and we will run the traps with Tang and Chee to see if Nyam will be okay here", and she smiled, just like an expectant mother-in-law.

So they waited for Chee to contact them, winding down from the melancholy of losing Willie. They still could hardly believe he was dead.

Three days later, a messenger came with a large packet that contained contracts for Udaa to review, prior to meeting with company principals. It was a pile-driving project on the Hong Kong waterfront, with Chinese- and Portuguese-speaking subcontractors. She was to report in three days' time to the vessel Fairwinds in Hong Kong. She was advised that she could bring a staff of two. The fee for her services was very lucrative.

Udaa reviewed the packet carefully. The contracts looked genuine, but this deal was all new to her. She looked up at Batu, Nyam and Onor.

"This is vintage Chee at work." She pulled passports for Batu and Nyam, and three prepaid airline tickets out of the packet. "Dalandzadgad, to Ulan Bator, to Hong Kong. He is very thorough, and everything appears legitimate. He does good work."

After long thought, Nyam asked if he could stay in Mongolia with Onor instead of making the trip with Udaa and Batu. Smiling, Udaa suggested that one asistant might be enough for this job. So Batu and Udaa prepared for the trip to Hong Kong, which included a haircut, suit and shoes for Batu. He felt like a different person, and practiced walking around the courtyard in his new shoes. The money was cleaned, dried, and repacked in the bottom of the battered suitcases that Udaa had used for years.

Batu and Nyam took a walk together, up on the hill behind the villa, and discussed their future.

Nyam asked, "Where do you think you will go?"

Batu dipped his head as he thought. "Maybe Lagos, Nigeria. Willie said it's wide open, and there's a spirit of optimism there. I could use some optimism, and it's warm there. I don't know about the horses in Nigeria, though."

Nyam was saddened by the thought of him leaving. "Let's keep in touch, and if either of us has problems, the other comes running, right?"

Batu nodded. "You know, a friend is someone you can go to when <u>he</u> is having trouble." They shook hands on it.

THE NEXT MORNING, AS they waited for the taxi to take them to the airport, Batu showed off his new suit, and danced a step or two in his new shoes, then confessed that he felt naked without a gun or a knife. The taxi came, and after emotional farewells, Udaa and Batu were on their way.

In the taxi he asked, "Is it true about the white streaming, when you are flying? I've never been on an airplane before."

She responded, "White streaming?"

"Yes," Batu answered, "Nyam said when you fly, all you see is white, streaming past the windows, like buttermilk on a glass. And you are pushed back in your seat for hours!"

Uda laughed, shaking her head. "It's nothing like that. The sensation is one of being suspended in air, and the view is beautiful."

Batu pondered this answer with a grimace. "I will get Nyam for that."

Her prophecy proved true, even in the commuter flight from Dalandzadgad to Mongolia's capital, which only took a little over an hour. The aircraft was an ancient Russian model that was like a flying tractor, with mud on the passageway floor and the smell of livestock emanating from the back. Goats, Batu thought. He enjoyed the view immensely, in spite of the noise from the huge, rattling engines.

At Ulan Bator, they experienced the joys of airport food, declared "carry on only" and were underway again within an hour. The early start was paying off. Batu was relaxed in a window seat, enjoying the view and the quieter roar of the jet, thankful that Nyam's description of flying was not true. A little less than halfway into the four-hour flight, in good weather, Batu was fascinated to see the Great Wall of China, near the city of Yulin, east of Beijing. He smiled as he observed the wall, thinking about it being built to keep his forefathers out of China.

"It doesn't look like much," he muttered in typical Mongolian fashion. They were flying at thirty thousand feet.

Chapter 15
Hong Kong

They landed in Hong Kong in heavy rain, deplaned and passed through Customs and Immigration easily. Officials were used to Udaa passing through, and Batu was seen as just another helpful staff member. A limo driver was waiting for them in the passageway, holding a sign that said "Udaa" over his head. He even carried umbrellas for them to use. They were whisked to the Hong Kong waterfront, fighting the after-work traffic in the heavy rain.

At approximately 6:00 pm, Hong Kong time, the limo pulled up in front of the freighter Fairwinds, with the hailing port Melbourne stenciled on its transom.

"That flag, see the stars? That's the southern cross; Australian." Udaa offered.

Batu stared at the ship, It was big, rusty in places, and bore the scars of years of transport. He was amazed. This was all very new to him.

Udaa approached a non-descript sailor waiting at the boarding ramp, and said, "Permission to board, sir, we have been instructed to meet with the captain in the wardroom adjacent to the pilot house." She showed him the letter, trying to keep it dry under the umbrella.

The sailor glanced at the letter, looked at Udaa and Batu, and asked, "Only one aide?"

Udaa nodded, and the sailor said, "Please follow me." He turned and proceeded up the ramp, saying "Please stow the umbrellas as you board the ship. Bad luck, umbrellas on a ship."

Umbrellas folded, they climbed the steel stairway in the rain, and entered the pilothouse. The sailor entered first, followed by Udaa. Batu was last, looking around, and glanced down at his new shoes that had gotten wet. He hoped they weren't ruined, as his bad feet felt good in them. Feeling the presence of another person close to him, Batu looked up, into the smiling face of Willie "the Goat" Barron!

Batu was shocked and speechless. Willie had come back from the dead! Then Willie hugged his stunned friend. Batu remembered that Willie was a "hugger," which must be an American trait. Suddenly they were all laughing, and Willie was pounding him on the back, and introducing himself to Udaa.

Geo Chee, behind Willie, completed the introductions and explained, "Sorry for all the secrecy. We had to be careful of leaks, and we had to do some intricate maneuvering."

Batu touched Willie on the chest to make sure he was still real. He looked between Willie and Geo, asking, "But, but how . . . ?"

Chee continued, "The executions were a sham, of course, but it only had to work until we got him out. Sometimes Mongolia's isolation works for us. Also, we paid the right people. And Nyam is now free to stay in Mongolia as long as he wishes."

Willie was smoking a large Cuban cigar, and drinking — would you believe it? — scotch whiskey. The ship's captain, who had been introduced to them, was a good provider.

LATER, WILLIE AND BATU sat in the corner of the ship's wardroom, drinking scotch and catching up. Hearing Batu's story, Willie was amazed.

"I'm glad Nyam is okay, and is together with his woman again." He looked at the overhead pipes running in every direction. "Sounds like it was a double, double-cross with two factions cutting themselves in for all the money. They even recruited the Russian from Dansk to spy on me."

Batu asked, "Did your courier make it out okay? He was very clever. Also, I'm confused about the timing. How did they know to wait so long for us, for the money?"

Willie responded, "My guy just keyed on the URBAD guys. As long as they waited, he would stay in the bush. He has no nerves, he used to be a sniper. The URBAD guys must have had watchers, who, for money, reported "sightings" of you along the way. I used to do that in my business."

Batu, always quick, asked, "Used to?"

"Yep," Willie took an expansive puff on his cigar. "I have retired from the smuggling business, and I want to talk to you about that."

"Oh boy," thought Batu. *"Here we go again."*

Later, after a good dinner, Willie and Batu were sitting in deck chairs under an awning on the afterdeck. The view of Hong Kong across the water, with millions of lights glowing, was magnificent. Willie was in rare form, and Batu was enjoying every minute of it. It was like old times, except they were warm, well fed, and full of scotch.

"Christ," Willie was complaining, "that money you gave me smells like shit."

Batu asked innocently, "See any bugs on it?"

Willie shuddered, then sat up and grinned. "But enough of that," he said enthusiastically, "Let's talk about the future."

Batu looked at him and cocked his head, thinking, *"What now?"*

"I'm out of the old business. It was a good career," Willie said, sounding like a retired investment banker. "The future, Batu, is in the most used <u>legal</u> drug in the world today, and its use is growing. The potential is phenomenal."

Batu was now a little worried by all this zeal. "So what now?" he asked.

"Coffee!" Willie yelled, rising to his feet, throwing out his arms. "What a great, natural, habit-forming drug! Coffee is our future, Batu, and horses."

"Horses?" Batu asked, now interested.

By now, Willie was almost jumping up and down. Batu was glad they were alone on the afterdeck.

"I have found, my friend, the perfect place for us. And, I have taken it upon myself to liquidate my, er, assets, and make some investments."

"Would you explain?" Batu insisted, "You're sounding like a fucking lawyer — those are your words, by the way."

Willie laughed. He loved these exchanges with Batu. "I bought a coffee plantation on Tanna Island in Vanuatu. It comes with processing facilities, in an old Catholic Church, I might add, on the main island of Efate, near Port Vila, the capital. It's warm, green, and beautiful." Then he paused for dramatic effect, before continuing, "And, for you, I have purchased a stable of racehorses from Melbourne that we will train at Port Vila; and — would you believe? There is a racetrack within walking distance of the coffee processing plant."

"We can grow and process coffee, train horses, and enter the Melbourne Cup every year during hurricane season — and take the Aussie's money! And it's all legal, no chance of prison!"

Willie sobered, "I hope you will join me in this venture. Even now, Cheech is on his way to Vanuatu to set things up. I brokered him out of URBAD, but he was a hard sell. He wanted to be a lifeguard in California. I guess he saw some old "Baywatch" tapes. I wanted Nyam to come too, but it sounds like he will be busy."

Willie turned the burner up. "Twelve days sailing time to Vanuatu. If you can believe it, the country was jointly run by the French and English before it gained independence. I figure that left them so confused, they will let us in, no problem." Then the kicker: "Tell you what, I'll throw in the money you returned as a signing bonus."

He watched nervously as Batu looked at him thoughtfully. Batu wrinkled his nose, curled his upper lip up, and said "I don't want your stinking money, but count me in."

Epilog
18 Months Later

Ex-Sergeant Tugso Erdene, Uno, no longer in the Mongolian Army, but still sporting his gunfighter mustache, drove his taxi around the edge of Housgol Lake near his hometown of Hanh. He thought of the tourists that he had to deal with in the summer months, and the weather in the winter. He said to himself, *"I hate this damn job,"* and he dreamed of the cobbler shop he would have some day, making excellent custom shoes and boots that would beat out the discount stores, even in Mongolia. But with the money he made, it would be a long time coming.

As he pulled in at his house, he noticed a large truck parked in front. His wife was standing on the porch with a curious look on her face.

She approached him and said, "That truck has a huge box for you. It must be a mistake."

But the paperwork said it was for him and the trucker helped him unload. Uno was completely amazed. Box after box came off the truck.

The boxes contained equipment for a complete cobbler shop, including a sewing machine made in Germany, lasts, leathers, polish, brushes — everything for a cobbler shop. The trucker said everything was paid for, gave him an envelope, and left.

Uno opened the envelope to find only two pictures, nothing else. One picture showed the big one, Nyam. He was standing with a beautiful lady, and they were holding a baby. The other picture showed Batu and Willie, who he thought was dead, posing with two beautiful horses at a racetrack. In the background he saw the huge Russian they called Cheech, holding a saddle, almost unrecognizable, as he'd never seen him smile before.

Uno vowed that they would all get new boots, every year.

THE END

Acknowledgements

Publishing a book is a lot more than writing the story.

Sometimes you're lucky to have people around you who make your work look good. I'm lucky. One person who helped with this book is Joni Reid, my wife, lover, best friend and inspiration. She helped put it all together, the organizing, editing, help with rewriting, plot and character adjustments, and computer complexities that go with publishing.

I also am indebted to Audrey Kunde for the cover art. Audrey is one of my nieces, whip smart and a great artist. It's great to have a large, talented family.

Thanks also to the many friends, relatives and other pre-readers who reviewed and critiqued my drafts, and provided so much encouragement and inspiration. The writing community is a large and generous group!

Don't miss out!

Visit the website below and you can sign up to receive emails whenever Jerry Reid publishes a new book. There's no charge and no obligation.

https://books2read.com/r/B-A-TTMN-FPSWB

BOOKS 2 READ

Connecting independent readers to independent writers.

Did you love *Escape from Mongolia*? Then you should read *Hunter's Eyes*[1] by Jerry Reid!

From a young age, Trosclair dreamed of having a plantation-style house on the high ground west of Iberia, where he could sight his rifle on the fence line, sit on the porch with the love of his life, and listen to the mockingbirds. When the war came, his skills from the oil fields, shrimp boats, moonshine stills and poaching served him well. Trosclair found himself in the United States Marine Corps, leading a Force Recon team in Vietnam. The loss of two team members leads Trosclair to revenge, where he nearly loses his life, but instead finds love and riches. Returning home, he finds his

----

1. https://books2read.com/u/3n20rK

2. https://books2read.com/u/3n20rK

land in Louisiana and shares his wealth with the friends from the battlefields. He has Mae Lee, the light of his life and kindred spirit, and the future looks bright. On the eve of their wedding day, while fishing for shrimp for the reception, a breaking wave over the transom caused the boat to broach. Trosclair regained consciousness to find Mae Lee missing. She was gone. Trosclair survived but was devastated by the loss, and disappears. As months go by, strange incidents occur which cause friends and family to think Mae Lee may be alive, and has been taken for a reason. Trosclair must be found. The search for Trosclair and Mae Lee is on, from faraway Alaska, to the San Juan Islands of the Pacific Northwest, to Panama. Trosclair and his friends take on old enemies, forge new alliances, and go farther than they thought possible.

Also by Jerry Reid

Hunter's Eyes
Escape from Mongolia
Madison Teagarden's Quest

About the Author

Jerry Reid's passion is exploring inland waterways, bays and estuaries in his 32-foot shallow-draft sloop, observing wildlife in quiet anchorages while eating good food, drinking box wine, and reading good books with his first mate Joni. He sails out of Bellingham, Washington.

Jerry's comments: Thank you for looking at this book. The characters in my stories are largely drawn from my experiences, ranging from digging ditches in Texas, a hitch in the Marine Corps, flying charter in the mountains of the Pacific Northwest, building a 40-foot sailboat in my backyard, to sailing on a 10-year circumnavigation and visiting 40 countries. The characters also come from friends, relatives and acquaintances — so look for yourself, you may be in this book.

The appeal to me of writing adventure stories is the opportunity to join with these characters, some far away or no longer with us — to enjoy their company once more in my memories, and see what they do this time. Stay safe in these times, and enjoy life. - Jerry

About the Publisher

Oxbow Publishing prints adventure stories and character-driven tales. If you have comments on this book or other Oxbow Publishing books, you can reach us at oxbowcompany@gmail.com.

Oxbow Publishing has made possible these books by Jerry Reid:

Hunter's Eyes, Escape from Mongolia, and Madison Teagarden's Quest: Pursuit of a Madman on Vanuatu.

Soon to be published: The Spice Hound.

www.ingramcontent.com/pod-product-compliance
Lightning Source LLC
Chambersburg PA
CBHW021402150726
47989CB00005B/2366